PUFFIN BOOKS

NEW TREASURE SEEKERS

The six Bastable children are Oswald, Dora, Dicky, Alice, H.O. and Noël – all familiar to children who have read *The Story of the Treasure Seekers* and *The Wouldbegoods* (both available in Puffin), or who have seen the recent television series about their exploits.

With imagination and enthusiasm they fill their free time with excitement and fun, though things don't always turn out as they plan. Like the time they unwittingly help a young couple to elope and like the time they try to alleviate a friend's poverty by letting some rooms in her house – to an escaped lunatic! Any other adventurers might retire after such mishaps, especially when they cap them all by getting arrested – but the Bastables don't. To them, it's all good fun and usually in a good cause. Their escapades will entertain present-day children of nine and over as much as their counterparts in 1904, when this book was first published.

E. NESBIT

NEW
TREASURE
SEEKERS

PUFFIN BOOKS

Puffin Books, Penguin Books Ltd, Harmondsworth, Middlesex, England
Penguin Books, 625 Madison Avenue, New York, New York 10022, U.S.A.
Penguin Books Australia Ltd, Ringwood, Victoria, Australia
Penguin Books Canada Ltd, 2801 John Street, Markham, Ontario, Canada L3R 1B4
Penguin Books (N.Z.) Ltd, 182–190 Wairau Road, Auckland 10, New Zealand

First published 1904
Published in Puffin Books 1982
Reprinted 1982

Printed and bound in Great Britain by
Cox & Wyman Ltd, Reading
Filmset in Baskerville by
Rowland Phototypesetting Ltd,
Bury St Edmunds, Suffolk

CONTENTS

THE ROAD TO ROME; OR,
THE SILLY STOWAWAY

WE Bastables have only two uncles, and neither of them are our own natural-born relatives. One is a great-uncle, and the other is the uncle from his birth of Albert, who used to live next door to us in the Lewisham Road. When we first got to know him (it was over some baked potatoes, and is quite another story) we called him Albert-next-door's-Uncle, and then Albert's uncle for short. But Albert's uncle and my father joined in taking a jolly house in the country, called the Moat House, and we stayed there for our summer holidays; and it was there, through an accident to a pilgrim with peas in his shoes – that's another story too – that we found Albert's uncle's long-lost love; and as she was very old indeed – twenty-six next birthday – and he was ever so much older in the vale of years, he had to get married almost directly, and it was fixed for about Christmastime. And when our holidays came the whole six of us went down to the Moat House with Father and Albert's uncle. We never had a Christmas in the country before. It was simply ripping. And the long-lost love – her name was Miss Ashleigh, but we were allowed to call her Aunt Margaret even before the wedding made it really legal for us to do so – she and her jolly clergyman brother used to come over, and sometimes we went to the Cedars, where they live, and we had games and charades, and hide-and-seek, and Devil in the Dark, which is a game girls pretend to like, and very few do really, and crackers and a Christmas-tree for the village children, and everything you can jolly well think of.

And all the time, whenever we went to the Cedars, there was all sorts of silly fuss going on about the beastly wedding; boxes coming from London with hats and jackets in, and wedding presents – all glassy and silvery, or else brooches and chains – and clothes sent down from London to choose from. I can't think how a lady can want so many petticoats and boots and things just because she's going to be married. No man would think of getting twenty-four shirts and twenty-four waistcoats, and so on, just to be married in.

'It's because they're going to Rome, I think,' Alice said, when we talked it over before the fire in the kitchen the day Mrs Pettigrew went to see her aunt, and we were allowed to make toffee. 'You see, in Rome you can only buy Roman clothes, and I think they're all stupid bright colours – at least I know the sashes are. You stir now, Oswald. My face is all burnt black.'

Oswald took the spoon, though it was really not his turn by three; but he is one whose nature is so that he cannot make a fuss about little things – and he knows he can make toffee.

'Lucky hounds,' H.O. said, 'to be going to Rome. I wish I was.'

'Hounds isn't polite, H.O., dear,' Dora said; and H.O. said –

'Well, lucky bargees, then.'

'It's the dream of my life to go to Rome,' Noël said. Noël is our poet brother. 'Just think of what the man says in the "Roman Road". I wish they'd take me.'

'They won't,' Dicky said. 'It costs a most awful lot. I heard Father saying so only yesterday.'

'It would only be the fare,' Noël answered; 'and I'd go third, or even in a cattle-truck, or a luggage van. And when I got there I could easily earn my own living. I'd make ballads and sing them in the streets. The Italians would give me lyres – that's the Italian kind of shilling, they spell it with an *i*. It shows how poetical they are out there, their calling it that.'

'But you couldn't make Italian poetry,' H.O. said, staring at Noël with his mouth open.

'Oh, I don't know so much about that,' Noël said. 'I could jolly soon learn anyway, and just to begin with I'd do it in English. There are sure to be some people who would understand. And if they didn't, don't you think their warm Southern hearts would be touched to see a pale, slender, foreign figure singing plaintive ballads in an unknown tongue? I do. Oh! they'd chuck along the lyres fast enough – they're not hard and cold like North people. Why, every one here is a brewer, or a baker, or a banker, or a butcher, or something dull. Over there they're all bandits, or vine-yardiners, or play the guitar, or something, and they crush the red grapes and dance and laugh in the sun – you know jolly well they do.'

'This toffee's about done,' said Oswald suddenly. 'H.O., shut your silly mouth and get a cupful of cold water.' And then, what with dropping a little of the toffee into the water to see if it was ready, and pouring some on a plate that wasn't buttered and not being able to get it off again when it was cold without breaking the plate, and the warm row there was about its being one of the best dinner-service ones, the wild romances of Noël's poetical intellect went out of our heads altogether; and it was not till later, and when deep in the waters of affliction, that they were brought back to us.

Next day H.O. said to Dora, 'I want to speak to you all by yourself and me.' So they went into the secret staircase that creaks and hasn't been secret now for countless years; and after that Dora did some white sewing she wouldn't let us look at, and H.O. helped her.

'It's another wedding present, you may depend,' Dicky

said – 'a beastly surprise, I shouldn't wonder.' And no more was said. The rest of us were busy skating on the moat, for it was now freezing hard. Dora never did care for skating; she says it hurts her feet.

And now Christmas and Boxing Day passed like a radiating dream, and it was the wedding-day. We all had to go to the bride's mother's house before the wedding, so as to go to church with the wedding party. The girls had always wanted to be somebody's bridesmaids, and now they were – in white cloth coats like coachmen, with lots of little capes, and white beaver bonnets. They didn't look so bad, though rather as if they were in a Christmas card; and their dresses were white silk like pocket-handkerchiefs under the long coats. And their shoes had real silver buckles our great Indian uncle gave them. H.O. went back just as the waggonette was starting, and came out with a big brown-paper parcel. We thought it was the secret surprise present Dora had been making, and, indeed, when I asked her she nodded. We little recked what it really was, or how our young brother was going to shove himself forward once again. He *will* do it. Nothing you say is of any lasting use.

There were a great many people at the wedding – quite crowds. There was lots to eat and drink, and though it was all cold, it did not matter, because there were blazing fires in every fireplace in the house, and the place all decorated with holly and mistletoe and things. Every one seemed to enjoy themselves very much, except Albert's uncle and his blushing bride; and they looked desperate. Every one said how sweet she looked, but Oswald thought she looked as if she didn't like being married as much as she expected. She was not at all a blushing bride really; only the tip of her nose got pink, because it was rather cold in the church. But she is very jolly.

Her reverend but nice brother read the marriage service.

He reads better than any one I know, but he is not a bit of a prig really, when you come to know him.

When the rash act was done Albert's uncle and his bride went home in a carriage all by themselves, and then we had the lunch and drank the health of the bride in real champagne, though Father said we kids must only have just a taste. I'm sure Oswald, for one, did not want any more; one taste was quite enough. Champagne is like soda-water with medicine in it. The sherry we put sugar in once was much more decent.

Then Miss Ashleigh – I mean Mrs Albert's uncle – went away and took off her white dress and came back looking much warmer. Dora heard the housemaid say afterwards that the cook had stopped the bride on the stairs with 'a basin of hot soup, that would take no denial, because the bride, poor dear young thing, not a bite or sup had passed her lips that day'. We understood then why she had looked so unhappy. But Albert's uncle had had a jolly good breakfast – fish and eggs and bacon and three goes of marmalade. So it was not hunger made him sad. Perhaps he was thinking what a lot of money it cost to be married and go to Rome.

A little before the bride went to change, H.O. got up and reached his brown-paper parcel from under the sideboard and sneaked out. We thought he might have let us see it given, whatever it was. And Dora said she had understood he meant to; but it was his secret.

The bride went away looking quite comfy in a furry cloak, and Albert's uncle cheered up at the last and threw off the burden of his cares and made a joke. I forget what it was; it wasn't a very good one, but it showed he was trying to make the best of things.

Then the Bridal Sufferers drove away, with the luggage on a cart – heaps and heaps of it, and we all cheered and threw rice and slippers. Mrs Ashleigh and some other old ladies cried.

And then every one said, 'What a pretty wedding!' and began to go. And when our waggonette came round we all began to get in. And suddenly Father said –

'Where's H.O.?' And we looked round. He was in absence.

'Fetch him along sharp – some of you,' Father said; 'I don't want to keep the horses standing here in the cold all day.'

So Oswald and Dicky went to fetch him along. We thought he might have wandered back to what was left of the lunch – for he is young and he does not always know better. But he was not there, and Oswald did not even take a crystallized fruit in passing. He might easily have done this, and no one would have minded, so it would not have been wrong. But it would have been ungentlemanly. Dicky did not either. H.O. was not there.

We went into the other rooms, even the one the old ladies were crying in, but of course we begged their pardons. And at last into the kitchen, where the servants were smart with white bows and just sitting down to their dinner, and Dicky said –

'I say, cookie love, have you seen H.O.?'

'Don't come here with your imperence!' the cook said, but she was pleased with Dicky's unmeaning compliment all the same.

'I see him,' said the housemaid. 'He was colloguing with the butcher in the yard a bit since. He'd got a brown-paper parcel. Perhaps he got a lift home.'

So we went and told Father, and about the white present in the parcel.

'I expect he was ashamed to give it after all,' Oswald said, 'so he hooked off home with it.'

And we got into the waggonette.

'It wasn't a present, though,' Dora said; 'it was a different kind of surprise – but it really is a secret.'

Our good Father did not command her to betray her young brother.

But when we got home H.O. wasn't there. Mrs Pettigrew hadn't seen him, and he was nowhere about. Father biked back to the Cedars to see if he'd turned up. No. Then all the gentlemen turned out to look for him through the length and breadth of the land.

'He's too old to be stolen by gipsies,' Alice said.

'And too ugly,' said Dicky.

'Oh *don't!*' said both the girls; 'and now when he's lost, too!'

We had looked for a long time before Mrs Pettigrew came in with a parcel she said the butcher had left. It was not addressed, but we knew it was H.O.'s, because of the label on the paper from the shop where Father gets his shirts. Father opened it at once.

Inside the parcel we found H.O.'s boots and braces, his best hat and his chest-protector. And Oswald felt as if we had found his skeleton.

'Any row with any of you?' Father asked. But there hadn't been any.

'Was he worried about anything? Done anything wrong, and afraid to own up?'

We turned cold, for we knew what he meant. That parcel was so horribly like the lady's hat and gloves that she takes off on the seashore and leaves with a letter saying it has come to this.

'*No, no*, NO, NO!' we all said. 'He was perfectly jolly all the morning.'

Then suddenly Dicky leaned on the table and one of H.O.'s boots toppled over, and there was something white inside. It was a letter. H.O. must have written it before we left home. It said –

DEAR FATHER AND EVERY ONE, – I am going to be a Clown. When I am rich and reveared I will come back rolling.

Your affectionate son,
HORACE OCTAVIUS BASTABLE.

'Rolling?' Father said.

'He means rolling in money,' Alice said. Owsald noticed that every one round the table where H.O.'s boots were dignifiedly respected as they lay, was a horrid pale colour, like when the salt is thrown into snapdragons.

'Oh dear!' Dora cried, 'that was it. He asked me to make him a clown's dress and keep it deeply secret. He said he wanted to surprise Aunt Margaret and Albert's uncle. And I didn't think it was wrong,' said Dora, screwing up her face; she then added, 'Oh dear, oh dear, oh oh!' and with these concluding remarks she began to howl.

Father thumped her on the back in an absent yet kind way.

'But where's he gone?' he said, not to any one in particular. 'I saw the butcher; he said H.O. asked him to take a parcel home and went back round the Cedars.'

Here Dicky coughed and said –

'I didn't think he meant anything, but the day after Noël was talking about singing ballads in Rome, and getting poet's lyres given him, H.O. did say if Noël had been really keen on the Roman lyres and things he could easily have been a stowaway, and gone unknown.'

'A stowaway!' said my father, sitting down suddenly and hard.

'In Aunt Margaret's big dress basket – the one she let him hide in when we had hide-and-seek there. He talked a lot about it after Noël had said that about the lyres – and the Italians being so poetical, you know. You remember that day we had toffee.'

My father is prompt and decisive in action, so is his eldest son.

'I'm off to the Cedars,' he said.

'Do let me come, Father,' said the decisive son. 'You may want to send a message.'

So in a moment Father was on his bike and Oswald on the step – a dangerous but delightful spot – and off to the Cedars.

'Have your teas; and *don't* any more of you get lost, and don't sit up if we're late,' Father howled to them as we rushed away. How glad then the thoughtful Oswald was that he was the eldest. It was very cold in the dusk on the bicycle, but Oswald did not complain.

At the Cedars my father explained in a few manly but well-chosen words, and the apartment of the dear departed bride was searched.

'Because,' said my father, 'if H.O. really was little ass enough to get into that basket, he must have turned out something to make room for himself.'

Sure enough, when they came to look, there was a great bundle rolled in a sheet under the bed – all lace things and petticoats and ribbons and dressing-gowns and ladies' flummery.

'If you will put the things in something else, I'll catch the express to Dover and take it with me,' Father said to Mrs Ashleigh; and while she packed the things he explained to some of the crying old ladies who had been unable to leave off, how sorry he was that a son of his – but you know the sort of thing.

Oswald said: 'Father, I wish you'd let me come too. I won't be a bit of trouble.'

Perhaps it was partly because my father didn't want to let me walk home in the dark, and he didn't want to worry the Ashleighs any more by asking them to send me home. He said this was why, but I hope it was his loving wish to have his prompt son, so like himself in his decisiveness, with him.

We went.

It was an anxious journey. We knew how far from pleased the bride would be to find no dressing-gowns and ribbons, but only H.O. crying and cross and dirty, as likely as not, when she opened the basket at the hotel at Dover.

Father smoked to pass the time, but Oswald had not so much as a peppermint or a bit of Spanish liquorice to help him through the journey. Yet he bore up.

When we got out at Dover there were Mr and Mrs Albert's uncle on the platform.

'Hullo,' said Albert's uncle. 'What's up? Nothing wrong at home, I hope.'

'We've only lost H.O.,' said my father. 'You don't happen to have him with you?'

'No; but you're joking,' said the bride. 'We've lost a dress-basket.'

Lost a dress-basket! The words struck us dumb, but my father recovered speech and explained. The bride was very glad when we said we had brought her ribbons and things, but we stood in anxious gloom, for now H.O. was indeed lost. The dress-basket might be on its way to Liverpool, or rocking on the Channel, and H.O. might never be found again. Oswald did not say these things. It is best to hold your jaw when you want to see a thing out, and are liable to be sent to bed at a strange hotel if any one happens to remember you.

Then suddenly the station master came with a telegram.

It said: 'A dress-basket without label at Cannon Street detained for identification suspicious sounds from inside detain inquirers dynamite machine suspected.'

He did not show us this till my father had told him about H.O., which it took some time for him to believe, and then he did and laughed, and said he would wire them to get the dynamite machine to speak, and if so, to take it out and keep it till its father called for it.

So back we went to London, with hearts a little lighter, but not gay, for we were a very long time from the last things we had had to eat. And Oswald was almost sorry he had not taken those crystallized fruits.

It was quite late when we got to Cannon Street, and we went straight into the cloak-room, and there was the man in charge, a very jolly chap, sitting on a stool. And there was H.O., the guilty stowaway, dressed in a red-and-white clown's dress, very dusty, and his face as dirty as I have ever seen it, sitting on some one else's tin box, with his feet on some body's else's portmanteau, eating bread and cheese, and drinking ale out of a can.

My father claimed him at once, and Oswald identified the basket. It was very large. There was a tray on the top with hats in it, and H.O. had this on top of him. We all went to bed in Cannon Street Hotel. My father said nothing to H.O. that night. When we were in bed I tried to get H.O. to tell me all about it, but he was too sleepy and cross. It was the beer and the knocking about in the basket, I suppose. Next day we went back to the Moat House, where the raving anxiousness of the others had been cooled the night before by a telegram from Dover.

My father said he would speak to H.O. in the evening. It is very horrid not to be spoken to at once and get it over. But H.O. certainly deserved something.

It is hard to tell this tale, because so much of it happened all at once but at different places. But this is what H.O. said to us about it. He said –

'Don't bother – let me alone.'

But we were all kind and gentle, and at last we got it out of him what had happened. He doesn't tell a story right from the beginning like Oswald and some of the others do, but from his disjunctured words the author has made the following narration. This is called editing, I believe.

'It was all Noël's fault,' H.O. said; 'what did he want to go jawing about Rome for? – and a clown's as good as a beastly poet, anyhow! You remember that day we made toffee? Well, I thought of it then.'

'You didn't tell us.'

'Yes, I did. I half told Dicky. He never said don't, or you'd better not, or gave me any good advice or anything. It's his fault as much as mine. Father ought to speak to him to-night the same as me – and Noël, too.'

We bore with him just then because we wanted to hear the story. And we made him go on.

'Well – so I thought if Noël's a cowardy custard I'm not – and I wasn't afraid of being in the basket, though it was quite dark till I cut the air-holes with my knife in the railway van. I think I cut the string off the label. It fell off afterwards, and I saw it through the hole, but of course I couldn't say anything. I thought they'd look after their silly luggage better than that. It was all their fault I was lost.'

'Tell us how you did it, H.O. dear,' Dora said; 'never mind about it being everybody else's fault.'

'It's yours as much as any one's, if you come to that,' H.O. said. 'You made me the clown dress when I asked you. You never said a word about not. So there!'

'Oh, H.O., you *are* unkind!' Dora said. 'You know you said it was for a surprise for the bridal pair.'

'So it would have been, if they'd found me at Rome, and I'd popped up like what I meant to – like a jack-in-the-box – and said, "Here we are again!" in my clown's clothes, at them. But it's all spoiled, and Father's going to speak to me this evening.' H.O. sniffed every time he stopped speaking. But we did not correct him then. We wanted to hear about everything.

'Why didn't you tell me straight out what you were going to do?' Dicky asked.

'Because you'd jolly well have shut me up. You always do if I want to do anything you haven't thought of yourself.'

'What did you take with you, H.O.?' asked Alice in a hurry, for H.O. was now sniffing far beyond a whisper.

'Oh, I'd saved a lot of grub, only I forgot it at the last. It's under the chest of drawers in our room. And I had my knife – and I changed into the clown's dress in the cupboard at the Ashleighs – over my own things because I thought it would be cold. And then I emptied the rotten girl's clothes out and hid them – and the top-hatted tray I just put it on a chair near, and I got into the basket, and I lifted the tray up over my head and sat down and fitted it down over me – it's got webbing bars, you know, across it. And none of you would ever have thought of it, let alone doing it.'

'I should hope not,' Dora said, but H.O. went on unhearing.

'I began to think perhaps I wished I hadn't directly they strapped up the basket. It was beastly hot and stuffy – I had to cut an airhole in the cart, and I cut my thumb; it was so bumpety. And they threw me about as if I was coals – and wrong way up as often as not. And the train was awful wobbly, and I felt so sick, and if I'd had the grub I couldn't have eaten it. I had a bottle of water. And that was all right till I dropped the cork, and I couldn't find it in the dark till the water got upset, and then I found the cork that minute.

'And when they dumped the basket on to the platform I was so glad to sit still a minute without being jogged I nearly went to sleep. And then I looked out, and the label was off, and lying close by. And then some one gave the basket a kick – big brute, I'd like to kick him! – and said, "What's this here?" And I daresay I did squeak – like a rabbit-noise, you know – and then some one said, "Sounds like live-stock, don't it? No label." And he was standing on the label all the time. I saw the string sticking out under his nasty boot. And then they trundled me off somewhere, on a wheelbarrow it felt like, and dumped me down again in a dark place – and I couldn't see anything more.'

'I wonder,' said the thoughtful Oswald, 'what made them think you were a dynamite machine?'

'Oh, that was awful!' H.O. said. 'It was my watch. I wound it up, just for something to do. You know the row it makes since it was broken, and I heard some one say, "Shish! what's that?" and then, "Sounds like an infernal machine" – don't go shoving me, Dora, it was him said it, not me – and then, "If I was the inspector I'd dump it down in the river, so I would. Any way, let's shift it." But the other said, "Let well alone," so I wasn't dumped any more. And they fetched another man, and there was a heap of jaw, and I heard them say "Police", so I let them have it.'

'What *did* you do?'

'Oh, I just kicked about in the basket, and I heard them all start off, and I shouted, "Hi, here! let me out, can't you!"'

'And did they?'

'Yes, but not for ever so long, I had to jaw at them through the cracks of the basket. And when they opened it there was quite a crowd, and they laughed ever so, and gave me bread and cheese, and said I was a plucky youngster – and I am, and I do wish Father wouldn't put things off so. He might just as well have spoken to me this morning. And I can't see I've done anything so awful – and it's all your faults for not looking after me. Aren't I your little brother? and it's your duty to see I do what's right. You've told me so often enough.'

These last words checked the severe reprimand trembling on the hitherto patient Oswald's lips. And then H.O. began to cry, and Dora nursed him, though generally he is much too big for this and knows it. And he went to sleep on her lap, and said he didn't want any dinner.

When it came to Father's speaking to H.O. that evening it never came off, because H.O. was ill in bed, not sham, you know, but real, send-for-the-doctor ill. The doctor said it was fever from chill and excitement, but I think myself it was very likely the things he ate at lunch, and the shaking up, and then the bread and cheese, and the beer out of a can.

He was ill a week. When he was better, not much was said. My father, who is the justest man in England, said the boy had been punished enough – and so he had, for he missed going to the pantomime, and to 'Shock-Headed Peter' at the Garrick Theatre, which is far and away the best play that ever was done, and quite different from any other acting I ever saw. They are exactly like real boys; I think they must have been reading about us. And he had to take a lot of the filthiest medicine I ever tasted. I wonder if Father told the doctor to make it nasty on purpose? A woman would have directly, but gentlemen are not generally so sly. Any way, you live and learn. None of us would now ever consent to be a stowaway, no matter who wanted us to, and I don't think H.O.'s very likely to do it again.

The only *meant* punishment he had was seeing the clown's dress burnt before his eyes by Father. He had bought it all with his own saved-up money, red trimmings and all.

Of course, when he got well we soon taught him not to say again that it was any of our faults. As he owned himself, he *is* our little brother, and we are not going to stand that kind of cheek from *him*.

THE CONSCIENCE-PUDDING

IT was Christmas, nearly a year after Mother died. I cannot write about Mother – but I will just say one thing. If she had only been away for a little while, and not for always, we shouldn't have been so keen on having a Christmas. I didn't understand this then, but I am much older now, and I think it was just because everything was so different and horrid we felt we *must* do something; and perhaps we were not particular enough *what*. Things make you much more unhappy when you loaf about than when you are doing events.

Father had to go away just about Christmas. He had heard that his wicked partner, who ran away with his money, was in France, and he thought he could catch him, but really he was in Spain, where catching criminals is never practised. We did not know this till afterwards.

Before Father went away he took Dora and Oswald into his study, and said –

'I'm awfully sorry I've got to go away, but it is very serious business, and I must go. You'll be good while I'm away, kiddies, won't you?'

We promised faithfully. Then he said –

'There are reasons – you wouldn't understand if I tried to tell you – but you can't have much of a Christmas this year. But I've told Matilda to make you a good plain pudding. Perhaps next Christmas will be brighter.'

(It was; for the next Christmas saw us the affluent nephews and nieces of an Indian uncle – but that is quite another story, as good old Kipling says.)

When Father had been seen off at Lewisham Station with

his bags, and a plaid rug in a strap, we came home again, and it was horrid. There were papers and things littered all over his room where he had packed. We tidied the room up – it was the only thing we could do for him. It was Dicky who accidentally broke his shaving-glass, and H.O. made a paper boat out of a letter we found out afterwards Father particularly wanted to keep. This took us some time, and when we went into the nursery the fire was black out, and we could not get it alight again, even with the whole *Daily Chronicle*. Matilda, who was our general then, was out, as well as the fire, so we went and sat in the kitchen. There is always a good fire in kitchens. The kitchen hearthrug was not nice to sit on, so we spread newspapers on it.

It was sitting in the kitchen, I think, that brought to our minds my father's parting words – about the pudding, I mean.

Oswald said, 'Father said we couldn't have much of a Christmas for secret reasons, and he said he had told Matilda to make us a plain pudding.'

The plain pudding instantly cast its shadow over the deepening gloom of our young minds.

'I wonder *how* plain she'll make it?' Dicky said.

'As plain as plain, you may depend,' said Oswald. 'A here-am-I-where-are-you pudding – that's her sort.'

The others groaned, and we gathered closer round the fire till the newspapers rustled madly.

'I believe I could make a pudding that *wasn't* plain, if I tried,' Alice said. 'Why shouldn't we?'

'No chink,' said Oswald, with brief sadness.

'How much would it cost?' Noël asked, and added that Dora had twopence and H.O. had a French halfpenny.

Dora got the cookery-book out of the dresser drawer, where it lay doubled up among clothes-pegs, dirty dusters, scallop shells, string, penny novelettes, and the dining-room corkscrew. The general we had then – it seemed as if she did all the cooking on the cookery-book instead of on the baking-board, there were traces of so many bygone meals upon its pages.

'It doesn't say Christmas pudding at all,' said Dora.

'Try plum,' the resourceful Oswald instantly counselled.

Dora turned the greasy pages anxiously.

'"Plum-pudding, 518.

'"A rich, with flour, 517.

'"Christmas, 517.

'"Cold brandy sauce for, 241.

'We shouldn't care about that, so it's no use looking.

'"Good without eggs, 518.

'"Plain, 518."

'We don't want *that* anyhow. "Christmas 517" – that's the one.'

It took her a long time to find the page. Oswald got a shovel of coals and made up the fire. It blazed up like the devouring elephant the *Daily Telegraph* always calls it. Then Dora read –

'"Christmas plum-pudding. Time six hours."'

'To eat it in?' said H.O.

'No, silly! to make it.'

'Forge ahead, Dora,' Dicky replied.

Dora went on –

'"2072. One pound and a half of raisins; half a pound of currants; three quarters of a pound of breadcrumbs; half a pound of flour; three-quarters of a pound of beef suet; nine eggs; one wine glassful of brandy; half a pound of citron and orange peel; half a nutmeg; and a little ground ginger." I wonder *how* little ground ginger.'

'A teacupful would be enough, I think,' Alice said; 'we must not be extravagant.'

'We haven't got anything yet to be extravagant *with*,' said Oswald, who had toothache that day. 'What would you do with the things if you'd got them?'

'You'd "chop the suet as fine as possible" – I wonder how fine that is?' replied Dora and the book together – '"and mix it with the breadcrumbs and flour; add the currants washed and dried."'

'Not starched, then,' said Alice.

'"The citron and orange peel cut into thin slices" – I wonder what they call thin? Matilda's thin bread-and-butter is quite different from what I mean by it – "and the raisins stoned and divided." How many heaps would you divide them into?'

'Seven, I suppose,' said Alice; 'one for each person and one for the pot – I mean pudding.'

'"Mix it all well together with the grated nutmeg and ginger. Then stir in nine eggs well beaten, and the brandy" – we'll leave that out, I think – "and again mix it thoroughly together that every ingredient may be moistened; put it into a buttered mould, tie over tightly, and boil for six hours. Serve it ornamented with holly and brandy poured over it."'

'I should think holly and brandy poured over it would be simply beastly,' said Dicky.

'I expect the book knows. I daresay holly and water would do as well though. "This pudding may be made a month before" – it's no use reading about that though, because we've only got four days to Christmas.'

'It's no use reading about any of it,' said Oswald, with thoughtful repeatedness, 'because we haven't got the things, and we haven't got the coin to get them.'

'We might get the tin somehow,' said Dicky.

'There must be lots of kind people who would subscribe to a Christmas pudding for poor children who hadn't any,' Noël said.

'Well, I'm going skating at Penn's,' said Oswald. 'It's no use thinking about puddings. We must put up with it plain.'

So he went, and Dicky went with him.

When they returned to their home in the evening the fire had been lighted again in the nursery, and the others were just having tea. We toasted our bread-and-butter on the bare side, and it gets a little warm among the butter. This is called French toast. 'I like English better, but it is more expensive,' Alice said –

'Matilda is in a frightful rage about your putting those coals on the kitchen fire, Oswald. She says we shan't have enough to last over Christmas as it is. And Father gave her a talking to before he went about them – asked her if she ate them, she says – but I don't believe he did. Anyway, she's locked the coal-cellar door, and she's got the key in her pocket. I don't see how we can boil the pudding.'

'What pudding?' said Oswald dreamily. He was thinking of a chap he had seen at Penn's who had cut the date 1899 on the ice with four strokes.

'*The* pudding,' Alice said. 'Oh, we've had such a time, Oswald! First Dora and I went to the shops to find out exactly what the pudding would cost – it's only two and elevenpence halfpenny, counting in the holly.'

'It's no good,' Oswald repeated; he is very patient and will say the same thing any number of times. 'It's no good. You know we've got no tin.'

'Ah,' said Alice, 'but Noël and I went out, and we called at some of the houses in Granville Park and Dartmouth Hill – and we got a lot of sixpences and shillings, besides pennies, and one old gentleman gave us half-a-crown. He was so nice. Quite bald, with a knitted red and blue waistcoat. We've got eight-and-sevenpence.'

Oswald did not feel quite sure Father would like us to go asking for shillings and sixpences, or even half-crowns from strangers, but he did not say so. The money had been asked for and got, and it couldn't be helped – and perhaps he wanted the pudding – I am not able to remember exactly why he did not speak up and say, 'This is wrong', but anyway he didn't.

Alice and Dora went out and bought the things next morning. They bought double quantities, so that it came to five shillings and elevenpence, and was enough to make a noble pudding. There was a lot of holly left over for decorations. We used very little for the sauce. The money that was left we spent very anxiously in other things to eat, such as dates and figs and toffee.

We did not tell Matilda about it. She was a red-haired girl, and apt to turn shirty at the least thing.

Concealed under our jackets and overcoats, we carried the parcels up to the nursery, and hid them in the treasure-chest we had there. It was the bureau drawer. It was locked up afterwards because the treacle got all over the green baize and the little drawers inside it while we were waiting to begin to make the pudding. It was the grocer told us we ought to put treacle in the pudding, and also about not so much ginger as a teacupful.

When Matilda had begun to pretend to scrub the floor (she pretended this three times a week so as to have an excuse not to let us in the kitchen, but I know she used to read novelettes most of the time, because Alice and I had a squint through the window more than once), we barricaded the nursery door and set to work. We were very careful to be quite clean. We washed our hands as well as the currants. I have sometimes thought we did not get all the soap off the currants. The pudding smelt like a washing-day when the time came to cut it open. And we washed a corner of the table to chop the suet on. Chopping suet looks easy till you try.

Father's machine he weighs letters with did to weigh out the things. We did this very carefully, in case the grocer had not done so. Everything was right except the raisins. H.O. had carried them home. He was very young then, and there was a hole in the corner of the paper bag and his mouth was sticky.

Lots of people have been hanged to a gibbet in chains on evidence no worse than that, and we told H.O. so till he cried. This was good for him. It was not unkindness to H.O., but part of our duty.

Chopping suet as fine as possible is much harder than any one would think, as I said before. So is crumbling bread – especially if your loaf is new, like ours was. When we had done them the breadcrumbs and the suet were both very large and lumpy, and of a dingy grey colour, something like pale slate pencil.

They looked a better colour when we had mixed them with the flour. The girls had washed the currants with Brown Windsor soap and the sponge. Some of the currants got inside the sponge and kept coming out in the bath for days afterwards. I see now that this was not quite nice. We cut the candied peel as thin as we wish people would cut our bread-and-butter. We tried to take the stones out of the raisins, but they were too sticky, so we just divided them up in seven lots. Then we mixed the other things in the wash-hand basin from the spare bedroom that was always spare. We each put in our own lot of raisins and turned it all into a pudding-basin, and tied it up in one of Alice's pinafores, which was the nearest thing to a proper pudding-cloth we could find – at any rate clean. What was left sticking to the wash-hand basin did not taste so bad.

'It's a little bit soapy,' Alice said, 'but perhaps that will boil out; like stains in table-cloths.'

It was a difficult question how to boil the pudding. Matilda proved furious when asked to let us, just because some one had happened to knock her hat off the scullery door and Pincher had got it and done for it. However, part of the embassy nicked a saucepan while the others were being told what Matilda thought about the hat, and we got hot water out of the bath-room and made it boil over our nursery fire. We put the pudding in – it was now getting on towards the hour of tea – and let it boil. With some exceptions – owing to the fire going down, and Matilda not hurrying up with coals – it boiled for an hour and a quarter. Then Matilda came suddenly in and said, 'I'm not going to have you messing about in here with my saucepans'; and she tried to take it off the fire. You will see that we couldn't stand this; it was not likely. I do not remember who it was that told her to mind her own business, and I think I have forgotten who caught hold of her first to make her chuck it. I am sure no needless violence was used. Anyway, while the struggle progressed, Alice and Dora took the saucepan away and put it in the boot-cupboard under the stairs and put the key in their pocket.

This sharp encounter made every one very hot and cross. We got over it before Matilda did, but we brought her round before bedtime. Quarrels should always be made up before bedtime. It says so in the Bible. If this simple rule was followed there would not be so many wars and martyrs and law suits and inquisitions and bloody deaths at the stake.

All the house was still. The gas was out all over the house except on the first landing, when several darkly shrouded figures might have been observed creeping downstairs to the kitchen.

On the way, with superior precaution, we got out our saucepan. The kitchen fire was red, but low; the coal-cellar was locked, and there was nothing in the scuttle but a little coal-dust and the piece of brown paper that is put in to keep the coals from tumbling out through the bottom where the hole is. We put the saucepan on the fire and plied it with fuel – two *Chronicles*, a *Telegraph*, and two *Family Herald* novelettes were burned in vain. I am almost sure the pudding did not boil at all that night.

'Never mind,' Alice said. 'We can each nick a piece of coal every time we go into the kitchen to-morrow.'

This daring scheme was faithfully performed, and by night we had nearly half a waste-paper basket of coal, coke, and cinders. And in the depth of night once more we might have been observed, this time with our collier-like waste-paper basket in our guarded hands.

There was more fire left in the grate that night, and we fed it with the fuel we had collected. This time the fire blazed up, and the pudding boiled like mad. This was the time it boiled two hours – at least I think it was about that, but we dropped asleep on the kitchen tables and dresser. You dare not be lowly in the night in the kitchen, because of the beetles. We were aroused by a horrible smell. It was the pudding-cloth burning. All the water had secretly boiled itself away. We filled it up at once with cold, and the saucepan cracked. So we cleaned it and put it back on the shelf and took another and went to bed. You see what a lot of trouble we had over the pudding. Every evening till Christmas, which had now become only the day after to-morrow, we sneaked down in the inky midnight and boiled that pudding for as long as it would.

On Christmas morning we chopped the holly for the sauce, but we put hot water (instead of brandy) and moist sugar. Some of them said it was not so bad. Oswald was not one of these.

Then came the moment when the plain pudding Father had ordered smoked upon the board. Matilda brought it in and went away at once. She had a cousin out of Woolwich Arsenal to see her that day, I remember. Those far-off days are quite distinct in memory's recollection still.

Then we got out our own pudding from its hiding-place and gave it one last hurried boil – only seven minutes, because of the general impatience which Oswald and Dora could not cope with.

We had found means to secrete a dish, and we now tried to dish the pudding up, but it stuck to the basin, and had to be dislodged with the chisel. The pudding was horribly pale. We poured the holly sauce over it, and Dora took up the knife and was just cutting it when a few simple words from H.O. turned us from happy and triumphing cookery artists to persons in despair.

He said: 'How pleased all those kind ladies and gentlemen would be if they knew *we* were the poor children they gave the shillings and sixpences and things for!'

We all said, '*What?*' It was no moment for politeness.

'I say,' H.O. said, 'they'd be glad if they knew it was us was enjoying the pudding, and not dirty little, really poor children.'

'You should say "you were", not "you was",' said Dora, but it was as in a dream and only from habit.

'Do you mean to say' – Oswald spoke firmly, yet not angrily – 'that you and Alice went and begged for money for poor children, and then *kept* it?'

'We didn't keep it,' said H.O., 'we spent it.'

'We've kept the *things*, you little duffer!' said Dicky, looking at the pudding sitting alone and uncared for on its dish. 'You begged for money for poor children, and then *kept* it. It's stealing, that's what it is. I don't say so much about you – you're only a silly kid – but Alice knew better. Why did you do it?'

He turned to Alice, but she was now too deep in tears to get a word out.

H.O. looked a bit frightened, but he answered the question. We have taught him this. He said –

'I thought they'd give us more if I said poor children than if I said just us.'

'*That*'s cheating,' said Dicky – 'downright beastly, mean, low cheating.'

'I'm not,' said H.O.; 'and you're another.' Then he

began to cry too. I do not know how the others felt, but I understand from Oswald that he felt that now the honour of the house of Bastable had been stamped on in the dust, and it didn't matter what happened. He looked at the beastly holly that had been left over from the sauce and was stuck up over the pictures. It now appeared hollow and disgusting, though it had got quite a lot of berries, and some of it was the varied kind – green and white. The figs and dates and toffee were set out in the doll's dinner service. The very sight of it all made Oswald blush sickly. He owns he would have liked to cuff H.O., and, if he did for a moment wish to shake Alice, the author, for one, can make allowances.

Now Alice choked and spluttered, and wiped her eyes fiercely, and said, 'It's no use ragging H.O. It's my fault. I'm older than he is.'

H.O. said, 'It couldn't be Alice's fault. I don't see as it was wrong.'

'That, not as,' murmured Dora, putting her arm round the sinner who had brought this degrading blight upon our family tree, but such is girls' undetermined and affectionate silliness. 'Tell sister all about it, H.O. dear. Why couldn't it be Alice's fault?'

H.O. cuddled up to Dora and said snufflingly in his nose –

'Because she hadn't got nothing to do with it. I collected it all. She never went into one of the houses. She didn't want to.'

'And then took all the credit of getting the money,' said Dicky savagely.

Oswald said, 'Not much *credit*,' in scornful tones.

'Oh, you are *beastly*, the whole lot of you, except Dora!' Alice said, stamping her foot in rage and despair. 'I tore my frock on a nail going out, and I didn't want to go back, and I got H.O. to go to the houses alone, and I waited for him

34

outside. And I asked him not to say anything because I didn't want Dora to know about the frock – it's my best. And *I* don't know what he said inside. He never told me. But I'll bet anything he didn't *mean* to cheat.'

'You *said* lots of kind people would be ready to give money to get pudding for poor children. So I asked them to.'

Oswald, with his strong right hand, waved a wave of passing things over.

'We'll talk about that another time,' he said; 'just now we've got weightier things to deal with.'

He pointed to the pudding, which had grown cold during the conversation to which I have alluded. H.O. stopped crying, but Alice went on with it. Oswald now said –

'We're a base and outcast family. Until that pudding's out of the house we shan't be able to look any one in the face. We must see that that pudding goes to poor children – not grisling, grumpy, whiney-piney, pretending poor children – but real poor ones, just as poor as they can stick.'

'And the figs too – and the dates,' said Noël, with regretting tones.

'Every fig,' said Dicky sternly. 'Oswald is quite right.'

This honourable resolution made us feel a bit better. We hastily put on our best things, and washed ourselves a bit, and hurried out to find some really poor people to give the pudding to. We cut it in slices ready, and put it in a basket with the figs and dates and toffee. We would not let H.O. come with us at first because he wanted to. And Alice would not come because of him. So at last we had to let him. The excitement of tearing into your best things heals the hurt that wounded honour feels, as the poetry writer said – or at any rate it makes the hurt feel better.

We went out into the streets. They were pretty quiet – nearly everybody was eating its Christmas dessert. But presently we met a woman in an apron. Oswald said very politely –

'Please, are you a poor person?' And she told us to get along with us.

The next we met was a shabby man with a hole in his left boot.

Again Oswald said, 'Please, are you a poor person, and have you any poor little children?'

The man told us not to come any of our games with him, or we should laugh on the wrong side of our faces. We went on sadly. We had no heart to stop and explain to him that we had no games to come.

The next was a young man near the Obelisk. Dora tried this time.

She said, 'Oh, if you please we've got some Christmas pudding in this basket, and if you're a poor person you can have some.'

'Poor as Job,' said the young man in a hoarse voice, and he had to come up out of a red comforter to say it.

We gave him a slice of the pudding, and he bit into it without thanks or delay. The next minute he had thrown the pudding slap in Dora's face, and was clutching Dicky by the collar.

'Blime if I don't chuck ye in the river, the whole bloomin' lot of you!' he exclaimed.

The girls screamed, the boys shouted, and though Oswald threw himself on the insulter of his sister with all his manly vigour, yet but for a friend of Oswald's, who is in the police, passing at that instant, the author shudders to think what might have happened, for he was a strong young man, and Oswald is not yet come to his full strength, and the Quaggy runs all too near.

Our policeman led our assailant aside, and we waited anxiously, as he told us to. After long uncertain moments the young man in the comforter loafed off grumbling, and our policeman turned to us.

'Said you give him a dollop o'pudding, and it tasted of soap and hair-oil.'

I suppose the hair-oil must have been the Brown Wind-soriness of the soap coming out. We were sorry, but it was still our duty to get rid of the pudding. The Quaggy was handy, it is true, but when you have collected money to feed poor children and spent it on pudding it is not right to throw that pudding in the river. People do not subscribe shillings and sixpences and half-crowns to feed a hungry flood with Christmas pudding.

Yet we shrank from asking any more people whether they were poor persons, or about their families, and still more from offering the pudding to chance people who might bite into it and taste the soap before we had time to get away.

It was Alice, the most paralysed with disgrace of all of us, who thought of the best idea.

She said, 'Let's take it to the workhouse. At any rate they're all poor there, and they mayn't go out without leave, so they can't run after us to do anything to us after the pudding. No one would give them leave to go out to pursue people who had brought them pudding, and wreck vengeance on them, and at any rate we shall get rid of the conscience-pudding – it's a sort of conscience-money, you know – only it isn't money but pudding.'

The workhouse is a good way, but we stuck to it, though very cold, and hungrier than we thought possible when we started, for we had been so agitated we had not even stayed to eat the plain pudding our good father had so kindly and thoughtfully ordered for our Christmas dinner.

The big bell at the workhouse made a man open the door to us, when we rang it. Oswald said (and he spoke because he is next eldest to Dora, and she had had jolly well enough of saying anything about pudding) – he said –

'Please we've brought some pudding for the poor people.'

He looked us up and down, and he looked at our basket, then he said: 'You'd better see the Matron.'

We waited in a hall, feeling more and more uncomfy, and less and less like Christmas. We were very cold indeed, especially our hands and our noses. And we felt less and less able to face the Matron if she was horrid, and one of us at least wished we had chosen the Quaggy for the pudding's long home, and made it up to the robbed poor in some other way afterwards.

Just as Alice was saying earnestly in the burning cold ear of Oswald, 'Let's put down the basket and make a bolt for it. Oh, Oswald, *let's*!' a lady came along the passage. She was very upright, and she had eyes that went through you like blue gimlets. I should not like to be obliged to thwart that lady if she had any design, and mine was opposite. I am glad this is not likely to occur.

She said, 'What's all this about a pudding?'

H.O. said at once, before we could stop him, 'They say I've stolen the pudding, so we've brought it here for the poor people.'

'No, we didn't!' 'That wasn't why!'

'The money was given!' 'It was meant for the poor!' 'Shut up, H.O.!' said the rest of us all at once.

Then there was an awful silence. The lady gimleted us again one by one with her blue eyes.

Then she said: 'Come into my room. You all look frozen.'

She took us into a very jolly room with velvet curtains and a big fire, and the gas lighted, because now it was almost dark, even out of doors. She gave us chairs, and Oswald felt as if his was a dock, he felt so criminal, and the lady looked so Judgular.

Then she took the arm-chair by the fire herself, and said, 'Who's the eldest?'

'I am,' said Dora, looking more like a frightened white rabbit than I've ever seen her.

'Then tell me all about it.'

Dora looked at Alice and began to cry. That slab of pudding in the face had totally unnerved the gentle girl. Alice's eyes were red, and her face was puffy with crying; but she spoke up for Dora and said –

'Oh, please let Oswald tell. Dora can't. She's tired with the long walk. And a young man threw a piece of it in her face, and –'

The lady nodded and Oswald began. He told the story from the very beginning, as he has always been taught to, though he hated to lay bare the family honour's wound before a stranger, however judgelike and gimlet-eyed.

He told all – not concealing the pudding-throwing, nor what the young man said about soap.

'So,' he ended, 'we want to give the conscience-pudding to you. It's like conscience-money – you know what that is, don't you? But if you really think it is soapy and not just the young man's horridness, perhaps you'd better not let them eat it. But the figs and things are all right.'

When he had done the lady said, for most of us were crying more or less –

'Come, cheer up! It's Christmas-time, and he's very little – your brother, I mean. And I think the rest of you seem pretty well able to take care of the honour of the family. I'll take the conscience-pudding off your minds. Where are you going now?'

'Home, I suppose,' Oswald said. And he thought how nasty and dark and dull it would be. The fire out most likely and Father away.

'And your father's not at home, you say,' the blue-gimlet lady went on. 'What do you say to having tea with me, and then seeing the entertainment we have got up for our old people?'

Then the lady smiled and the blue gimlets looked quite merry.

The room was so warm and comfortable and the invitation was the last thing we expected. It was jolly of her, I do think.

No one thought quite at first of saying how pleased we should be to accept her kind invitation. Instead we all just said 'Oh!' but in a tone which must have told her we meant 'Yes, please', very deeply.

Oswald (this has more than once happened) was the first to restore his manners. He made a proper bow like he has been taught, and said –

'Thank you very much. We should like it very much. It is very much nicer than going home. Thank you very much.'

I need not tell the reader that Oswald could have made up a much better speech if he had had more time to make it up in, or if he had not been so filled with mixed flusteredness and furification by the shameful events of the day.

We washed our faces and hands and had a first rate muffin and crumpet tea, with slices of cold meats, and many nice jams and cakes. A lot of other people were there, most of them people who were giving the entertainment to the aged poor.

After tea it was the entertainment. Songs and conjuring and a play called 'Box and Cox', very amusing, and a lot of throwing things about in it – bacon and chops and things – and nigger minstrels. We clapped till our hands were sore.

When it was over we said goodbye. In between the songs and things Oswald had had time to make up a speech of thanks to the lady.

He said –

'We all thank you heartily for your goodness. The entertainment was beautiful. We shall never forget your kindness and hospitableness.'

The lady laughed, and said she had been very pleased to have us. A fat gentleman said –

'And your teas? I hope you enjoyed those – eh?'

Oswald had not had time to make up an answer to that, so he answered straight from the heart, and said –

'Ra – *ther!*'

And every one laughed and slapped us boys on the back and kissed the girls, and the gentleman who played the bones in the nigger minstrels saw us home. We ate the cold pudding that night, and H.O. dreamed that something came to eat him, like it advises you to in the advertisements on the hoardings. The grown-ups said it was the pudding, but I don't think it could have been that, because, as I have said more than once, it was so very plain.

Some of H.O.'s brothers and sisters thought it was a judgement on him for pretending about who the poor children were he was collecting the money for. Oswald does not believe such a little boy as H.O. would have a real judgement made just for him and nobody else, whatever he did.

But it certainly is odd. H.O. was the only one who had bad dreams, and he was also the only one who got any of the things we bought with that ill-gotten money, because, you remember, he picked a hole in the raisin-paper as he was bringing the parcel home. The rest of us had nothing, unless you count the scrapings of the pudding-basin, and those don't really count at all.

ARCHIBALD THE UNPLEASANT

THE house of Bastable was once in poor, but honest, circs. That was when it lived in a semi-detached house in the Lewisham Road, and looked for treasure. There were six scions of the house who looked for it – in fact there were seven, if you count Father. I am sure he looked right enough, but he did not do it the right way. And we did. And so we found a treasure of a great-uncle, and we and Father went to live with him in a very affluent mansion on Blackheath – with gardens and vineries and pineries and everything jolly you can think of. And then, when we were no longer so beastly short of pocket-money, we tried to be good, and sometimes it came out right, and sometimes it didn't. Something like sums.

And then it was the Christmas holidays – and we had a bazaar and raffled the most beautiful goat you ever saw, and we gave the money to the poor and needy.

And then we felt it was time to do something new, because we were as rich as our worthy relative, the uncle, and our father – now also wealthy, at least, compared to what he used to be – thought right for us; and we were as good as we could be without being good for nothing and muffs, which I hope no one calling itself a Bastable will ever stoop to.

So then Oswald, so often the leader in hazardous enterprises, thought long and deeply in his interior self, and he saw that something must be done, because, though there was still the goat left over, unclaimed by its fortunate winner at the Bazaar, somehow no really fine idea seemed to come out of it, and nothing else was happening. Dora was getting a bit domineering, and Alice was too much taken up with trying to learn to knit. Dicky was bored and so was Oswald, and Noël was writing far more poetry than could be healthy for any poet, however young, and H.O. was simply a nuisance. His boots are always much louder when he is not amused, and that gets the rest of us into rows, because there are hardly any grown-up persons who can tell the difference between his boots and mine. Oswald decided to call a council (because even if nothing comes of a council it always means getting Alice to drop knitting, and making Noël chuck the poetical influences, that are no use and only make him silly), and he went into the room that is our room. It is called the common-room, like in colleges, and it is very different from the room that was ours when we were poor, but honest. It is a jolly room, with a big table and a big couch, that is most useful for games, and a thick carpet because of H.O.'s boots.

Alice was knitting by the fire; it was for Father, but I am sure his feet are not at all that shape. He has a high and beautifully formed instep like Oswald's. Noël was writing poetry, of course.

> *My dear sister sits*
> *And knits,*
> *I hope to goodness the stocking fits,*

was as far as he had got.

'It ought to be "my dearest sister" to sound right,' he said, 'but that wouldn't be kind to Dora.'

'Thank you,' said Dora. 'You needn't trouble to be kind to me, if you don't want to.'

'Shut up, Dora!' said Dicky, 'Noël didn't mean anything.'

'He never does,' said H.O., 'nor yet his poetry doesn't neither.'

'*And* his poetry doesn't *either*,' Dora corrected; 'and besides, you oughtn't to say that at all, it's unkind –'

'You're too jolly down on the kid,' said Dicky.

And Alice said, 'Eighty-seven, eighty-eight – oh, do be quiet half a sec.! – eighty-nine, ninety – now I shall have to count the stitches all over again!'

Oswald alone was silent and not cross. I tell you this to show that the sort of worryingness was among us that is catching, like measles. Kipling calls it the cameelious hump, and, as usual, that great and good writer is quite correct.

So Oswald said, 'Look here, let's have a council. It says in Kipling's book when you've got the hump go and dig till you gently perspire. Well, we can't do that, because it's simply pouring, but –'

The others all interrupted him, and said they hadn't got the hump and they didn't know what he meant. So he shrugged his shoulders patiently (it is not his fault that the others hate him to shrug his shoulders patiently) and he said no more.

Then Dora said, 'Oh, don't be so disagreeable, Oswald, for goodness' sake!'

I assure you she did, though he had done simply nothing.

Matters were in this cryptical state when the door opened and Father came in.

'Hullo, kiddies!' he remarked kindly. 'Beastly wet day, isn't it? And dark too, I can't think why the rain can't always come in term time. It seems a poor arrangement to have it in "vac.", doesn't it?'

I think every one instantly felt better. I know one of us did, and it was me.

Father lit the gas, and sat down in the armchair and took Alice on his knee.

'First,' he said, 'here is a box of chocs.' It was an extra big and beautiful one and Fuller's best. 'And besides the chocs., a piece of good news! You're all asked to a party at Mrs Leslie's. She's going to have all sorts of games and things, with prizes for every one, and a conjurer and a magic lantern.'

The shadow of doom seemed to be lifted from each young brow, and we felt how much fonder we were of each other than any one would have thought. At least Oswald felt this, and Dicky told me afterwards he felt Dora wasn't such a bad sort after all.

'It's on Tuesday week,' said Father. 'I see the prospect pleases. Number three is that your cousin Archibald has come here to stay a week or two. His little sister has taken it into her head to have whooping-cough. And he's down-stairs now, talking to your uncle.'

We asked what the young stranger was like, but Father did not know, because he and cousin Archibald's father had not seen much of each other for some years. Father said this, but we knew it was because Archibald's father hadn't bothered to see ours when he was poor and honest, but now he was the wealthy sharer of the red-brick, beautiful Black-heath house it was different. This made us not like Uncle Archibald very much, but we were too just to blame it on to young Archibald. All the same we should have liked him better if his father's previous career had not been of such a worldly and stuck-up sort. Besides, I do think Archibald is quite the most rotten sort of name. We should have called him Archie, of course, if he had been at all decent.

'You'll be as jolly to him as you can, I know,' Father said; 'he's a bit older than you, Oswald. He's not a bad-looking chap.'

Then Father went down and Oswald had to go with him, and there was Archibald sitting upright in a chair and talking to our Indian uncle as if he was some beastly grown-up. Our cousin proved to be dark and rather tall, and though he was only fourteen he was always stroking his lip to see if his moustache had begun to come.

Father introduced us to each other, and we said, 'How do

you do?' and looked at each other, and neither of us could think of anything else to say. At least Oswald couldn't. So then we went upstairs. Archibald shook hands with the others, and every one was silent except Dora, and she only whispered to H.O. to keep his feet still.

You cannot keep for ever in melancholy silence however few things you have to say, and presently some one said it was a wet day, and this well-chosen remark made us able to begin to talk.

I do not wish to be injurious to anybody, especially one who was a Bastable, by birth at least if not according to the nobler attributes, but I must say that Oswald never did dislike a boy so much as he did that young Archibald. He was as cocky as though he'd done something to speak of – been captain of his eleven, or passed a beastly exam., or something – but we never could find that he had done anything. He was always bragging about the things he had at home, and the things he was allowed to do, and all the things he knew all about, but he was a most untruthful chap. He laughed at Noël's being a poet – a thing we never do, because it makes him cry and crying makes him ill – and of course Oswald and Dicky could not punch his head in their own house because of the laws of hospitableness, and Alice stopped it at last by saying she didn't care if it was being a sneak, she would tell Father the very next time. I don't think she would have, because we made a rule, when we were poor and honest, not to bother Father if we could possibly help it. And we keep it up still. But Archibald didn't know that. Then this cousin, who is, I fear, the black sheep of the Bastables, and hardly worthy to be called one, used to pull the girls' hair, and pinch them at prayers when they could not call out or do anything to him back.

And he was awfully rude to the servants, ordering them about, and playing tricks on them, not amusing tricks like other Bastables might have done – such as booby-traps and

mice under dish-covers, which seldom leaves any lasting
ill-feeling – but things no decent boy would do – like hiding
their letters and not giving them to them for days, and then
it was too late to meet the young man the letter was from,
and squirting ink on their aprons when they were just going
to open the door, and once he put a fish-hook in the cook's
pocket when she wasn't looking. He did not do anything to
Oswald at that time. I suppose he was afraid. I just tell you
this to show you that Oswald didn't cotton to him for no
selfish reason, but because Oswald has been taught to feel
for others.

He called us all kids – and he was that kind of boy we
knew at once it was no good trying to start anything new
and jolly – so Oswald, ever discreet and wary, shut up
entirely about the council. We played games with him
sometimes, not really good ones, but Snap and Beggar my
Neighbour, and even then he used to cheat. I hate to say it
of one of our blood, but I can hardly believe he was. I think
he must have been changed at nurse like the heirs to
monarchies and dukeries.

Well, the days passed slowly. There was Mrs Leslie's
party shining starrishly in the mysteries of the future. Also
we had another thing to look forward to, and that was when
Archibald would have to go back to school. But we could
not enjoy that foreshadowing so much because of us having
to go back at nearly the same time.

Oswald always tries to be just, no matter how far from
easy, and so I will say that I am not quite sure that it was
Archibald that set the pipes leaking, but we were all up in
the loft the day before, snatching a golden opportunity to
play a brief game of robbers in a cave, while Archibald had
gone down to the village to get his silly hair cut. Another
thing about him that was not natural was his being always
looking in the glass and wanting to talk about whether
people were handsome or not; and he made as much fuss

about his ties as though he had been a girl. So when he was gone Alice said –

'Hist! The golden moment. Let's be robbers in the loft, and when he comes back he won't know where we are.'

'He'll hear us,' said Noël, biting his pencil.

'No, he won't. We'll be the Whispering Band of Weird Bandits. Come on, Noël; you can finish the poetry up here.'

'It's about *him*,' said Noël gloomily, 'when he's gone back to –' (Oswald will not give the name of Archibald's school for the sake of the other boys there, as they might not like everybody who reads this to know about there being a chap like him in their midst.) 'I shall do it up in an envelope and put a stamp on it and post it to him, and –'

'Haste!' cried Alice. 'Bard of the Bandits, haste while yet there's time.'

So we tore upstairs and put on our slippers and socks over them, and we got the high-backed chair out of the girls' bedroom, and the others held it steady while Oswald agilitively mounted upon its high back and opened the trap-door and got up into the place between the roof and the ceiling (the boys in *Stalky & Co.* found this out by accident, and they were surprised and pleased, but we have known all about it ever since we can remember).

Then the others put the chair back, and Oswald let down the rope ladder that we made out of bamboo and clothes-line after uncle told us the story of the missionary lady who was shut up in a rajah's palace, and some one shot an arrow to her with a string tied to it, and it might have killed her I should have thought, but it didn't, and she hauled in the string and there was a rope and a bamboo ladder, and so she escaped, and we made one like it on purpose for the loft. No one had ever told us not to make ladders.

The others came up by the rope-ladder (it was partly bamboo, but rope-ladder does for short) and we shut the trap-door down. It is jolly up there. There are two big cisterns, and one little window in a gable that gives you just enough light. The floor is plaster with wooden things going across, beams and joists they are called. There are some planks laid on top of these here and there. Of course if you walk on the plaster you will go through with your foot into the room below.

We had a very jolly game, in whispers, and Noël sat by the little window, and was quite happy, being the bandit bard. The cisterns are rocks you hide behind. But the jolliest part was when we heard Archibald shouting out, 'Hullo! kids, where are you?' and we all stayed as still as mice, and heard Jane say she thought we must have gone out. Jane was the one that hadn't got her letter, as well as having her apron inked all over.

Then we heard Archibald going all over the house looking for us. Father was at business and uncle was at his club. And we were *there*. And so Archibald was all alone. And we might have gone on for hours enjoying the spectacle of his confusion and perplexedness, but Noël happened to sneeze — the least thing gives him cold and he sneezes louder for his age than any one I know – just when Archibald was on the landing underneath. Then he stood there and said –

'I know where you are. Let me come up.'

We cautiously did not reply. Then he said:

'All right. I'll go and get the step-ladder.'

We did not wish this. We had not been told not to make rope-ladders, nor yet about not playing in the loft; but if he fetched the step-ladder Jane would know, and there are some secrets you like to keep to yourself.

So Oswald opened the trap-door and squinted down, and there was that Archibald with his beastly hair cut. Oswald said –

'We'll let you up if you promise not to tell you've been up here.'

So he promised, and we let down the rope-ladder. And it will show you the kind of boy he was that the instant he had got up by it he began to find fault with the way it was made.

Then he wanted to play with the ball-cock. But Oswald knows it is better not to do this.

'I daresay *you're* forbidden,' Archibald said, 'little kids like you. But *I* know all about plumbing.'

And Oswald could not prevent his fiddling with the pipes and the ball-cock a little. Then we went down. All chance of further banditry was at an end. Next day was Sunday. The leak was noticed then. It was slow, but steady, and the plumber was sent for on Monday morning.

Oswald does not know whether it was Archibald who made the leak, but he does know about what came after.

I think our displeasing cousin found that piece of poetry that Noël was beginning about him, and read it, because he is a sneak. Instead of having it out with Noël he sucked up to him and gave him a sixpenny fountain-pen which Noël liked, although it is really no good for him to try to write poetry with anything but a pencil, because he always sucks whatever he writes with, and ink is poisonous, I believe.

Then in the afternoon he and Noël got quite thick, and went off together. And afterwards Noël seemed very peacocky about something, but he would not say what, and Archibald was grinning in a way Oswald would have liked to pound his head for.

Then, quite suddenly, the peaceable quietness of that happy Blackheath home was brought to a close by screams. Servants ran about with brooms and pails, and the water was coming through the ceiling of uncle's room like mad, and Noël turned white and looked at our unattractive cousin and said: 'Send him away.'

Alice put her arm round Noël and said: 'Do go, Archibald.'

But he wouldn't.

So then Noël said he wished he had never been born, and whatever would Father say.

'Why, what is it, Noël?' Alice asked that. 'Just tell us, we'll all stand by you. What's he been doing?'

'You won't let him do anything to me if I tell?'

'Tell tale tit,' said Archibald.

'He got me to go up into the loft and he said it was a secret, and would I promise not to tell, and I won't tell; only I've done it, and now the water's coming in.'

'You've done it? You young ass, I was only kidding you!' said our detestable cousin. And he laughed.

'I don't understand,' said Oswald. 'What did you tell Noël?'

'He can't tell you because he promised – and I won't – unless you vow by the honour of the house you talk so much about that you'll never tell I had anything to do with it.'

That will show you what he was. We had never mentioned the honour of the house except once quite at the beginning, before we knew how discapable he was of understanding anything, and how far we were from wanting to call him Archie.

We had to promise, for Noël was getting greener and more gurgly every minute, and at any moment Father or uncle might burst in foaming for an explanation, and none of us would have one except Noël, and him in this state of all-anyhow.

So Dicky said –

'We promise, you beast, you!' And we all said the same.

Then Archibald said, drawling his words and feeling for the moustache that wasn't there, and I hope he'll be quite old before he gets one –

'It's just what comes of trying to amuse silly little kids. I told the foolish little animal about people having arteries cut, and your having to cut the whole thing to stop the bleeding. And he said, "Was that what the plumber would do to the leaky pipe?" And how pleased your governor would be to find it mended. And then he went and did it.'

'You told me to,' said Noël, turning greener and greener.

'Go along with Alice,' said Oswald. 'We'll stand by you. And Noël, old chap, you must keep your word and not sneak about that sneaking hound.'

Alice took him away, and we were left with the horrid Archibald.

'Now,' said Oswald, 'I won't break my word, no more will the rest of us. But we won't speak another word to you as long as we live.'

'Oh, Oswald,' said Dora, 'what about the sun going down?'

'Let it jolly well go,' said Dicky in furiousness. 'Oswald didn't say we'd go on being angry for ever, but I'm with Oswald all the way. I won't talk to cads – no, not even before grown-ups. They can jolly well think what they like.'

After this no one spoke to Archibald.

Oswald rushed for a plumber, and such was his fiery eloquence he really caught one and brought him home. Then he and Dicky waited for Father when he came in, and they got him into the study, and Oswald said what they had all agreed on. It was this:

'Father, we are all most awfully sorry, but one of us has cut the pipe in the loft, and if you make us tell you any more it will not be honourable, and we are very sorry. Please, please don't ask who it was did it.'

Father bit his moustache and looked worried, and Dicky went on –

'Oswald has got a plumber and he is doing it now.'

Then Father said, 'How on earth did you get into the loft?'

And then of course the treasured secret of the rope-ladder had to be revealed. We had never been told not to make rope-ladders and go into the loft, but we did not try to soften the anger of our father by saying this. It would not have been any good either. We just had to stick it. And the punishment of our crime was most awful. It was that we weren't to go to Mrs Leslie's party. And Archibald was to go, because when Father asked him if he was in it with the rest of us, he said 'No.' I cannot think of any really gentle, manly, and proper words to say what I think about my unnatural cousin.

We kept our word about not speaking to him, and I think Father thought we were jealous because he was going to that conjuring, magic lantern party and we were not. Noël was the most unhappy, because he knew we were all being punished for what he had done. He was very affectionate and tried to write pieces of poetry to us all, but he was so unhappy he couldn't even write, and he went into the kitchen and sat on Jane's knee and said his head ached.

Next day it was the day of the party and we were plunged in gloom. Archibald got out his Etons and put his clean shirt ready, and a pair of flashy silk socks with red spots, and then he went into the bath-room.

Noël and Jane were whispering on the stairs. Jane came up and Noël went down. Jane knocked at the bath-room door and said –

'Here's the soap, Master Archerbald. I didn't put none in to-day.'

He opened the door and put out his hand.

'Half a moment,' said Jane, 'I've got something else in my hand.'

As she spoke the gas all over the house went down blue, and then went out. We held our breaths heavily.

'Here it is,' she said; 'I'll put it in your hand. I'll go down and turn off the burners and see about the gas. You'll be late, sir. If I was you I should get on a bit with the washing of myself in the dark. I daresay the gas'll be five or ten minutes, and it's five o'clock now.'

It wasn't, and of course she ought not to have said it, but it was useful all the same.

Noël came stumping up the stairs in the dark. He fumbled about and then whispered, 'I've turned the little white china knob that locks the bath-room door on the outside.'

The water was bubbling and hissing in the pipes inside, and the darkness went on. Father and uncle had not come in yet, which was a fortunate blessing.

'Do be quiet!' said Noël. 'Just you wait.'

We all sat on the stairs and waited. Noël said –

'Don't ask me yet – you'll see – you wait.'

And we waited, and the gas did not come back.

At last Archibald tried to come out – he thought he had washed himself clean, I suppose – and of course the door was fastened. He kicked and he hammered and he shouted, and we were glad.

At last Noël banged on the door and screamed through the keyhole –

'If we let you out will you let us off our promise not to tell about you and the pipes? We won't tell till you've gone back to school.'

He wouldn't for a long time, but at last he had to.

'I shan't ever come to your beastly house again,' he bellowed through the keyhole, 'so I don't mind.'

'Turn off the gas-burners then,' said Oswald, ever thoughtful, though he was still in ignorance of the beautiful truth.

Then Noël sang out over the stairs, 'Light up!' and Jane went round with a taper, and when the landing gas was lighted Noël turned the knob of the bath-room, and Archibald exited in his Indian red and yellow dressing-gown that he thought so much of. Of course we expected his face to be red with rage, or white with passion, or purple with mixed emotions, but you cannot think what our feelings were –

indeed, we hardly knew what they were ourselves – when we saw that he was not red or white or purple, but *black*. He looked like an uneven sort of bluish nigger. His face and hands were all black and blue in streaks, and so were the bits of his feet that showed between his Indian dressing-gown and his Turkish slippers.

The word 'Crikey' fell from more than one lip.

'What are you staring at?' he asked.

We did not answer even then, though I think it was less from keep-your-wordishness than amazement. But Jane did.

'Nyang, Nyang!' she uttered tauntingly. 'You thought it was soap I was giving you, and all the time it was Maple's dark bright navy-blue indelible dye – won't wash out.' She flashed a looking-glass in his face, and he looked and saw the depth of his dark bright navy-blueness.

Now, you may think that we shouted with laughing to see him done brown and dyed blue like this, but we did not. There was a spellbound silence. Oswald, I know, felt a quite uncomfortable feeling inside him.

When Archibald had had one good look at himself he did not want any more. He ran to his room and bolted himself in.

'*He* won't go to no parties,' said Jane, and she flounced downstairs.

We never knew how much Noël had told her. He is very young, and not so strong as we are, and we thought it better not to ask.

Oswald and Dicky and H.O. – particularly H.O. – told each other it served him right, but after a bit Dora asked Noël if he would mind her trying to get some of it off our unloved cousin, and he said 'No.'

But nothing would get it off him; and when Father came home there was an awful row. And he said we had disgraced ourselves and forgotten the duties of hospitality. We got it pretty straight, I can tell you. And we bore it all. I do not say we were martyrs to the honour of our house and to our plighted word, but I do say that we got it very straight indeed, and we did not tell the provocativeness we had had from our guest that drove the poet Noël to this wild and desperate revenge.

But some one told, and I have always thought it was Jane, and that is why we did not ask too many questions about what Noël had told her, because late that night Father came and said he now understood that we had meant to do right, except perhaps the one who cut the pipe with a chisel, and that must have been more silliness than naughtiness; and perhaps the being dyed blue served our cousin rather right. And he gave Archibald a few remarks in private, and when the dye began to come off – it was not a fast dye, though it said so on the paper it was wrapped in – Archibald, now a light streaky blue, really did seem to be making an effort to be something like decent. And when, now merely a pale grey, he had returned to school, he sent us a letter. It said:

My dear Cousins,

I think that I was beastlier than I meant to be, but I am not accustomed to young kids. And I think uncle was right, and the way you stand up for the honour of our house is not all nonsense, like I said it was. If we ever meet in the future life I hope you will not keep a down on me about things. I don't think you can expect me to say more. From your affectionate cousin,

Archibald Bastable.

So I suppose rays of remorse penetrated that cold heart, and now perhaps he will be a reformed Bastable. I am sure I hope so, but I believe it is difficult, if not impossible, for a leopard to change his skin.

Still, I remember how indelibly black he looked when he came out of the fatal bathroom; and it nearly all wore off. And perhaps spots on the honourable inside parts of your soul come off with time. I hope so. The dye never came off the inside of the bath though. I think that was what annoyed our good great-uncle the most.

OVER THE WATER TO CHINA

OSWALD is a very modest boy, I believe, but even he would not deny that he has an active brain. The author has heard both his father and Albert's uncle say so. And the most far-reaching ideas often come to him quite naturally – just as silly notions that aren't any good might come to you. And he had an idea which he meant to hold a council about with his brothers and sisters; but just as he was going to unroll his idea to them our father occurred suddenly in our midst and said a strange cousin was coming, and he came, and he was strange indeed! And when Fate had woven the threads of his dark destiny and he had been dyed a dark bright navy-blue, and had gone from our midst, Oswald went back to the idea that he had not forgotten. The words 'tenacious of purpose' mean sticking to things, and these words always make me think of the character of the young hero of these pages. At least I suppose his brothers Dicky and Noël and H.O. are heroes too, in a way, but somehow the author of these lines knows more about Oswald's inside realness than he does about the others. But I am getting too deep for words.

So Oswald went into the common-room. Every one was busy. Noël and H.O. were playing Halma. Dora was covering boxes with silver paper to put sweets in for a school treat, and Dicky was making a cardboard model of a new screw he has invented for ocean steamers. But Oswald did not mind interrupting, because Dora ought not to work too hard, and Halma always ends in a row, and I would rather not say what I think of Dicky's screw. So Oswald said –

'I want a council. Where's Alice?'

Every one said they didn't know, and they made haste to say that we couldn't have a council without her. But Oswald's determined nature made him tell H.O. to chuck that rotten game and go and look for her. H.O. is our youngest brother, and it is right that he should remember this and do as he was told. But he happened to be winning the beastly Halma game, and Oswald saw that there was going to be trouble – 'big trouble', as Mr Kipling says. And he was just bracing his young nerves for the conflict with H.O., because he was not going to stand any nonsense from his young brother about his not fetching Alice when he was jolly well told to, when the missing maiden bounced into the room bearing upon her brow the marks of ravaging agi-tatedness.

'Have any of you seen Pincher?' she cried, in haste.

We all said, 'No, not since last night.'

'Well, then, he's lost,' Alice said, making the ugly face that means you are going to blub in half a minute.

Every one had sprung to their feet. Even Noël and H.O. saw at once what a doddering game Halma is, and Dora and Dicky, whatever their faults, care more for Pincher than for boxes and screws. Because Pincher is our fox-terrier. He is of noble race, and he was ours when we were poor, lonely treasure-seekers and lived in humble hard-upness in the Lewisham Road.

To the faithful heart of young Oswald the Blackheath affluent mansion and all it contains, even the stuffed fox eating a duck in the glass case in the hall that he is so fond of, and even the council he wanted to have, seemed to matter much less than old Pincher.

'I want you all to let's go out and look for him,' said Alice, carrying out the meaning of the faces she had made and beginning to howl. 'Oh, Pincher, suppose something hap-pens to him; you might get my hat and coat, Dora. Oh, oh, oh!'

We all got our coats and hats, and by the time we were ready Alice had conquered it to only sniffing, or else, as Oswald told her kindly, she wouldn't have been allowed to come.

'Let's go on the Heath,' Noël said. 'The dear departed dog used to like digging there.'

So we went. And we said to every single person we met –

'Please have you seen a thoroughbred fox-terrier dog with a black patch over one eye, and another over his tail, and a tan patch on his right shoulder?' And every one said, 'No, they hadn't', only some had more polite ways of saying it than others. But after a bit we met a policeman, and he said, 'I see one when I was on duty last night, like what you describe, but it was at the end of a string. There was a young lad at the other end. The dog didn't seem to go exactly willing.'

He also told us the lad and the dog had gone over Greenwich way. So we went down, not quite so wretched in our insides, because now it seemed that there was some chance, though we wondered the policeman *could* have let Pincher go when he saw he didn't want to, but he said it wasn't his business. And now we asked every one if they'd seen a lad and a thoroughbred fox-terrier with a black patch, and cetera.

And one or two people said they had, and we thought it must be the same the policeman had seen, because they said, too, that the dog didn't seem to care about going where he was going.

So we went on and through the Park and past the Naval College, and we didn't even stop to look at that life-sized firm ship in the playground that the Naval Collegians have to learn about ropes and spars on, and Oswald would willingly give a year of his young life to have that ship for his very own.

And we didn't go into the Painted Hall either, because

our fond hearts were with Pincher, and we could not really have enjoyed looking at Nelson's remains, of the shipwrecks where the drowning people all look so dry, or even the pictures where young heroes are boarding pirates from Spain, just as Oswald would do if he had half a chance, with the pirates fighting in attitudes more twisted and Spanish than the pirates of any nation could manage even if they were not above it. It is an odd thing, but all those pictures are awfully bad weather – even the ones that are not shipwrecks. And yet in books the skies are usually a stainless blue and the sea is a liquid gem when you are engaged in the avocation of pirate-boarding.

The author is sorry to see that he is not going on with the story.

We walked through Greenwich Hospital and asked there if they have seen Pincher, because I heard Father say once that dogs are sometimes stolen and taken to hospitals and never seen again. It is wrong to steal, but I suppose the hospital doctors forget this because they are so sorry for the poor ill people and like to give them dogs to play with them and amuse them on their beds of anguish. But no one had seen our Pincher, who seemed to be becoming more dear to our hearts every moment.

When we got through the Hospital grounds – they are big and the buildings are big, and I like it all because there's so much room everywhere and nothing niggling – we got down to the terrace over the river, next to the Trafalgar Hotel. And there was a sailor leaning on the railings, and we asked him the usual question. It seems that he was asleep, but of course we did not know, or we would not have disturbed him. He was very angry, and he swore, and Oswald told the girls to come away; but Alice pulled away from Oswald and said,

'Oh, don't be so cross. Do tell us if you've seen our dog? He is –' and she recited Pincher's qualifications.

'Ho yes,' said the sailor – he had a red and angry face. 'I see 'im a hour ago 'long of a Chinaman. 'E crossed the river in a open boat. You'd best look slippy arter 'im.' He grinned and spat; he was a detestable character, I think. 'Chinamen puts puppy-dogs in pies. If 'e catches you three young chaps 'e'll 'ave a pie as'll need a big crust to cover it. Get along with your cheek!'

So we got along. Of course, we knew that the Chinese are not cannibals, so we were not frightened by that rot; but we knew, too, that the Chinese do really eat dogs, as well as rats and birds' nests and other disgraceful forms of eating.

H.O. was very tired, and he said his boots hurt him; and Noël was beginning to look like a young throstle – all eyes and beak. He always does when he is tired. The others were tired too, but their proud spirits would never have owned it. So we went round to the Trafalgar Hotel's boathouse, and there was a man in slippers, and we said could we have a boat, and he said he would send a boatman, and would we walk in?

We did, and we went through a dark room piled up to the ceiling with boats and out on to a sort of thing half like a balcony and half like a pier. And there were boats there too, far more than you would think any one could want; and then a boy came. We said we wanted to go across the river, and he said, 'Where to?'

'To where the Chinamen live,' said Alice.

'You can go to Millwall if you want to,' he said, beginning to put oars into the boat.

'Are there any Chinese people there?' Alice asked.

And the boy replied, 'I dunno.' He added that he supposed we could pay for the boat.

By a fortunate accident – I think Father had rather wanted to make up to us for our martyr-like enduring when our cousin was with us – we were fairly flush of chink. Oswald and Dicky were proudly able to produce handfuls of money; it was mostly copper, but it did not fail of its effect.

The boy seemed not to dislike us quite so much as before, and he helped the girls into the boat, which was now in the water at the edge of a sort of floating, unsteady raft, with openings in it that you could see the water through. The water was very rough, just like real sea, and not like a river at all. And the boy rowed; he wouldn't let us, although I can, quite well. The boat tumbled and tossed just like a sea-boat. When we were about half-way over, Noël pulled Alice's sleeve and said –

'Do I look very green?'

'You do rather, dear,' she said kindly.

'I feel much greener than I look,' said Noël. And later on he was not at all well.

The boy laughed, but we pretended not to notice. I wish I could tell you half the things we saw as our boat was pulled along through the swishing, lumpy water that turned into great waves after every steamer that went by. Oswald was quite fit, but some of the others were very silent. Dicky says he saw everything that Oswald saw, but I am not sure. There were wharves and engines, and great rusty cranes swinging giant's handfuls of iron rails about in the air, and once we passed a ship that was being broken up. All the wood was gone, and they were taking away her plates, and the red rust was running from her and colouring the water all round; it looked as though she was bleeding to death. I suppose it was silly to feel sorry for her, but I did. I thought how beastly it was that she would never go to sea again, where the waves are clean and green, even if no rougher than the black waves now raging around our staunch little bark. I never knew before what lots of kinds of ships there can be, and I think I could have gone on and on for ever and ever looking at the shapes of things and the colours they were, and dreaming about being a pirate, and things like that, but we had come some way; and now Alice said –

'Oswald, I think Noël will die if we don't make land soon.'

And indeed he had been rather bad for some time, only I thought it was kinder to take no notice.

So our ship was steered among other pirate craft, and moored at a landing-place where there were steps up.

Noël was now so ill that we felt we could not take him on a Chinese hunt, and H.O. had sneaked his boots off in the boat, and he said they hurt him too much to put them on again; so it was arranged that those two should sit on a dry corner of the steps and wait, and Dora said she would stay with them.

'I think we ought to go home,' she said. 'I'm quite sure Father wouldn't like us being in these wild, savage places. The police ought to find Pincher.'

But the others weren't going to surrender like that, especially as Dora had actually had the sense to bring a bag of biscuits, which all, except Noël, were now eating.

'Perhaps they ought, but they *won't*,' said Dicky. 'I'm boiling hot. I'll leave you my overcoat in case you're cold.'

Oswald had been just about to make the same manly proposal, though he was not extra warm. So they left their coats, and, with Alice, who would come though told not to, they climbed the steps, and went along a narrow passage and started boldly on the Chinese hunt. It was a strange sort of place over the river; all the streets were narrow, and the houses and the pavements and the people's clothes and the mud in the road all seemed the same sort of dull colour – a sort of brown-grey it was.

All the house doors were open, and you could see that the insides of the houses were the same colour as the outsides. Some of the women had blue, or violet or red shawls, and they sat on the doorsteps and combed their children's hair, and shouted things to each other across the street. They seemed very much struck by the appearance of the three travellers, and some of the things they said were not pretty.

That was the day when Oswald found out a thing that has often been of use to him in after-life. However rudely poor people stare at you they become all right instantly if you ask them something. I think they don't hate you so much when they've done something for you, if it's only to tell you the time or the way.

So we got on very well, but it does not make me comfortable to see people so poor and we have such a jolly house. People in books feel this, and I know it is right to feel it, but I hate the feeling all the same. And it is worse when the people are nice to you.

And we asked and asked and asked, but nobody had seen a dog or a Chinaman, and I began to think all was indeed lost, and you can't go on biscuits all day, when we went round a corner rather fast, and came slap into the largest woman I have ever seen. She must have been yards and yards round, and before she had time to be in the rage that we saw she was getting into, Alice said —

'Oh, I beg your pardon! I *am* so sorry, but we really didn't mean to! I *do* so hope we didn't hurt you!'

We saw the growing rage fade away, and she said, as soon as she got her fat breath —

'No 'arm done, my little dear. An' w'ere are you off to in such a 'urry?'

So we told her all about it. She was quite friendly, although so stout, and she said we oughtn't to be gallivanting about all on our own. We told her we were all right, though I own Oswald was glad that in the hurry of departing Alice hadn't had time to find anything smarter-looking to wear than her garden coat and grey Tam, which had been regretted by some earlier in the day.

'Well,' said the woman, 'if you go along this 'ere turning as far as ever you can go, and then take the first to the right and bear round to the left, and take the second to the right again, and go down the alley between the stumps, you'll come to Rose Gardens. There's often Chinamen about there. And if you come along this way as you come back, keep your eye open for me, and I'll arks some young chaps as I know as is interested like in dogs, and perhaps I'll have news for you.'

'Thank you very much,' Alice said, and the woman asked her to give her a kiss. Everybody is always wanting to kiss Alice. I can't think why. And we got her to tell us the way again, and we noticed the name of the street, and it was Nightingale Street, and the stairs where we had left the others was Bullamy's Causeway, because we have the true explorer's instincts, and when you can't blaze your way on trees with your axe, or lay crossed twigs like the gipsies do, it is best to remember the names of streets.

So we said goodbye, and went on through the grey-brown streets with hardly any shops, and those only very small and common, and we got to the alley all right. It was a narrow place between high blank brown-grey walls. I think by the smell it was gasworks and tanneries. There was hardly any one there, but when we got into it we heard feet running ahead of us, and Oswald said –

'Hullo, suppose that's some one with Pincher, and they've recognized his long-lost masters and they're making a bolt for it?'

And we all started running as hard as ever we could. There was a turn in the passage, and when we got round it we saw that the running was stopping. There were four or five boys in a little crowd round some one in blue – blue looked such a change after the muddy colour of everything in that dead Eastern domain – and when we got up, the person the blue was on was a very wrinkled old man, with a yellow wrinkled face and a soft felt hat and blue blouse-like coat, and I see that I ought not to conceal any longer from the discerning reader that it was exactly what we had been looking for. It was indeed a Celestial Chinaman in deep difficulties with these boys who were, as Alice said afterwards, truly fiends in mortal shape. They were laughing at the old Chinaman, and shouting to each other, and their language was of that kind I was sorry we had got Alice with us. But she told Oswald afterwards that she was so angry she did not know what they were saying.

'Pull his bloomin' pigtail,' said one of these outcasts from decent conduct.

The old man was trying to keep them off with both hands, but the hands were very wrinkled and trembly.

Oswald is grateful to his good father who taught him and Dicky the proper way to put their hands up. If it had not been for that, Oswald does not know what on earth would have happened, for the outcasts were five to our two, because no one could have expected Alice to do what she did.

Before Oswald had even got his hands into the position required by the noble art of self-defence, she had slapped the largest boy on the face as hard as ever she could – and she can slap pretty hard, as Oswald knows but too well – and she had taken the second-sized boy and was shaking him before Dicky could get his left in on the eye of the slapped assailant of the aged denizen of the Flowery East. The other three went for Oswald, but three to one is nothing to one who has hopes of being a pirate in his spare time when he grows up.

In an instant the five were on us. Dicky and I got in some good ones, and though Oswald cannot approve of my sister being in a street fight, he must own she was very quick and useful in pulling ears and twisting arms and slapping and pinching. But she had quite forgotten how to hit out from the shoulder like I have often shown her.

The battle raged, and Alice often turned the tide of it by a well-timed shove or nip. The aged Eastern leaned against the wall, panting and holding his blue heart with his yellow hand. Oswald had got a boy down, and was kneeling on him, and Alice was trying to pull off two other boys who had fallen on top of the fray, while Dicky was letting the fifth have it, when there was a flash of blue and another China-man dashed into the tournament. Fortunately this one was not old, and with a few well-directed, if foreign looking, blows he finished the work so ably begun by the brave Bastables, and next moment the five loathsome and youthful aggressors were bolting down the passage. Oswald and Dicky were trying to get their breath and find out exactly where they were hurt and how much, and Alice had burst out crying and was howling as though she would never stop. That is the worst of girls – they never can keep anything up. Any brave act they may suddenly do, when for a moment they forget that they have not the honour to be boys, is almost instantly made into contemptibility by a sudden attack of crybabyishness. But I will say no more: for she did strike the first blow, after all, and it did turn out that the boys had scratched her wrist and kicked her shins. These things make girls cry.

The venerable stranger from distance shores said a good deal to the other in what I suppose was the language used in China. It all sounded like 'hung' and 'li' and 'chi', and then the other turned to us and said –

'Nicee lilly girlee, same piecee flowelee, you takee my head to walkee on. This is alle samee my father first chop ancestor. Dirty white devils makee him hurt. You come alongee fightee ploper. Me likee you welly muchee.'

Alice was crying too much to answer, especially as she could not find her handkerchief. I gave her mine, and then she was able to say that she did not want to walk on anybody's head, and she wanted to go home.

'This not nicee place for lillee whitee girlee,' said the young Chinaman. His pigtail was thicker than his father's and black right up to the top. The old man's was grey at the beginning, but lower down it was black, because that part of it was not hair at all, but black threads and ribbons and odds and ends of trimmings, and towards the end both pigtails were greenish.

'Me lun backee takee him safee,' the younger of the Eastern adventurers went on, pointing to his father. 'Then me makee walkee all alonk you, takee you back same placee you comee from. Little white devils waitee for you on ce load. You comee with? Not? Lillee girlee not cly. John givee her one piecee pletty-pletty. Come makee talkee with the House Lady.'

I believe this is about what he said, and we understood that he wanted us to come and see his mother, and that he would give Alice something pretty, and then see us safe out of the horrible brown-grey country.

So we agreed to go with them, for we knew those five boys would be waiting for us on the way back, most likely with strong reinforcements. Alice stopped crying the minute she could – I must say she is better than Dora in that way – and we followed the Chinamen, who walked in single file like Indians, so we did the same, and talked to each other over our shoulders. Our grateful Oriental friends led us through a good many streets, and suddenly opened a door with a key, pulled us in, and shut the door. Dick thought of the kidnapping of Florence Dombey and good Mrs Brown, but Oswald had no such unnoble thoughts.

The room was small, and very, very odd. It was very dirty too, but perhaps it is not polite to say that. There was a sort of sideboard at one end of the room, with an embroidered dirty cloth on it, and on the cloth a bluey-white crockery image over a foot high. It was very fat and army and leggy, and I think it was an idol. The minute we got inside the young man lighted little brown sticks, and set them to burn in front of it. I suppose it was incense. There was a sort of long, wide, low sofa, without any arms or legs, and a table that was like a box, with another box in front of it for you to sit down on when you worked, and on the table were all sorts of tiny little tools – awls and brads they looked like – and pipe-stems and broken bowls of pipes and mouthpieces, for our rescued Chinaman was a pipe-mender by trade. There wasn't much else in the room except the smell, and that seemed to fill it choke-full. The smell seemed to have all sorts of things in it – glue and gun-powder, and white garden lilies and burnt fat, and it was not so easy to breathe as plain air.

Then a Chinese lady came in. She had green-grey trous-ers, shiny like varnish, and a blue gown, and her hair was pulled back very tight, and twisted into a little knob at the back.

She wanted to go down on the floor before Alice, but we wouldn't let her. Then she said a great many things that we feel sure were very nice, only they were in Chinese, so we could not tell what they were.

And the Chinaman said that his mother also wanted Alice to walk on her head – not Alice's own, of course, but the mother's.

I wished we had stayed longer, and tried harder to understand what they said, because it was an adventure, take it how you like, that we're not likely to look upon the like of again. Only we were too flustered to see this.

We said, 'Don't mention it', and things like that; and when Dicky said, 'I think we ought to be going', Oswald said so too.

Then they all began talking Chinese like mad, and the Chinese lady came back and suddenly gave Alice a parrot.

It was red and green, with a very long tail, and as tame as any pet fawn I ever read about. It walked up her arm and round her neck, and stroked her face with its beak. And it did not bite Oswald or Alice, or even Dicky, though they could not be sure at first that it was not going to.

We said all the polite things we could, and the old lady made thousands of hurried Chinese replies, and repeated many times, 'All litey, John', which seemed to be all the English she knew.

We never had so much fuss made over us in all our lives. I think it was that that upset our calmness, and seemed to put us into a sort of silly dream that made us not see what idiots we were to hurry off from scenes we should never again behold. So we went. And the youthful Celestial saw us safely to the top of Bullamy's Stairs, and left us there with the parrot and floods of words that seemed all to end in double 'e'.

We wanted to show him to the others, but he would not come, so we rejoined our anxious relations without him.

The scene of rejoinder was painful, at first because they were most frightfully sick at us having been such an age away; but when we let them look at the parrot, and told them about the fight, they agreed that it was not our fault, and we really had been unavoidably detained.

But Dora said, 'Well, you may say I'm always preaching, but I *don't* think Father would like Alice to be fighting street boys in Millwall.'

'I suppose *you'd* have run away and let the old man be killed,' said Dicky, and peace was not restored till we were nearly at Greenwich again.

We took the tram to Greenwich Station, and then we took a cab home (and well worth the money, which was all we now had got, except fourpence-halfpenny), for we were all dog-tired.

And dog-tired reminds me that we hadn't found Pincher, in spite of all our trouble.

Miss Blake, who is our housekeeper, was angrier than I have ever seen her. She had been so anxious that she had sent the police to look for us. But, of course, they had not found us. You ought to make allowances for what people do when they are anxious, so I forgive her everything, even what she said about Oswald being a disgrace to a respectable house. He owns we were rather muddy, owing to the fight.

And when the jaw was over and we were having tea – and there was meat to it, because we were as near starving as I ever wish to be – we all ate lots. Even the thought of Pincher could not thwart our bold appetites, though we kept saying, 'Poor old Pincher!' 'I do wish we'd found him', and things like that. The parrot walked about among the tea-things as tame as tame. And just as Alice was saying how we'd go out again to-morrow and have another try for our faithful hound there was a scratching at the door, and we rushed – and there was Pincher, perfectly well and mad with joy to see us.

H.O. turned an abrupt beetroot colour.

'Oh!' he said.

We said, 'What? Out with it.'

And though he would much rather have kept it a secret buried in his breast, we made him own that he had shut Pincher up yesterday in the empty rabbit-hutch when he was playing Zoological Gardens and forgotten all about it in the pleasures of our cousin having left us.

So we need not have gone over the water at all. But though Oswald pities all dumb animals, especially those helplessly shut in rabbit-hutches at the bottoms of gardens, he cannot be sorry that we had such a Celestial adventure and got hold of such a parrot. For Alice says that Oswald and Dicky and she shall have the parrot between them.

She is tremendously straight. I often wonder why she was made a girl. She's a jolly sight more of a gentleman than half the boys at our school.

THE YOUNG ANTIQUARIES

THIS really happened before Christmas, but many authors go back to bygone years for whole chapters, and I don't see why I shouldn't.

It was one Sunday – the Somethingth Sunday in Advent, I think – and Denny and Daisy and their father and Albert's uncle came to dinner, which is in the middle of the day on that day of rest and the same things to eat for grown-ups and us. It is nearly always roast beef and Yorkshire, but the puddings and vegetables are brightly variegated and never the same two Sundays running.

At dinner some one said something about the coat-of-arms that is on the silver tankards which once, when we were poor and honest, used to stay at the shop having the dents slowly taken out of them for months and months. But now they are always at home and are put at the four corners of the table every day, and any grown-up who likes can drink beer out of them.

After some talk of the sort you don't listen to, in which bends and lioncels and gules and things played a promising part, Albert's uncle said that Mr Turnbull had told him something about that coat-of-arms being carved on a bridge somewhere in Cambridgeshire, and again the conversation wandered into things like Albert's uncle had talked about to the Maidstone Antiquarian Society the day they came over to see his old house in the country and we arranged the time-honoured Roman remains for them to dig up. So, hearing the words king-post and mullion and moulding and underpin, Oswald said might we go; and we went, and took our dessert with us and had it in our own common-room, where you can roast chestnuts with a free heart and never mind what your fingers get like.

When first we knew Daisy we used to call her the White Mouse, and her brother had all the appearance of being one too, but you know how untruthful appearances are, or else it was that we taught him happier things, for he certainly turned out quite different in the end; and she was not a bad sort of kid, though we never could quite cure her of wanting to be 'ladylike' – that is the beastliest word there is, I think, and Albert's uncle says so, too. He says if a girl can't be a lady it's not worth while to be only like one – she'd better let it alone and be a free and happy bounder.

But all this is not what I was going to say, only the author does think of so many things besides the story, and some-times he puts them in. This is the case with Thackeray and the Religious Tract Society and other authors, as well as Mrs Humphrey Ward. Only I don't suppose you have ever heard of her, though she writes books that some people like very much. But perhaps they are her friends. I did not like the one I read about the Baronet. It was on a wet Sunday at the seaside, and nothing else in the house but Bradshaw and 'Elsie; or like a –' or I shouldn't have. But what really happened to us before Christmas is strictly the following narrative.

'I say,' remarked Denny, when he had burned his fingers with a chestnut that turned out a bad one after all – and such is life – and he had finished sucking his fingers and getting rid of the chestnut, 'about these antiquaries?'

'Well, what about them?' said Oswald. He always tries to be gentle and kind to Denny, because he knows he helped to make a man of the young Mouse.

'I shouldn't think,' said Denny, 'that it was so very difficult to be one.'

'I don't know,' said Dicky. 'You have to read very dull

books and an awful lot of them, and remember what you read, what's more.'

'I don't think so,' said Alice. 'That girl who came with the antiquities – the one Albert's uncle said was up-holstered in red plush like furniture – *she* hadn't read anything, you bet.'

Dora said, 'You ought not to bet, especially on Sunday,' and Alice altered it to 'You may be sure.'

'Well, but what then?' Oswald asked Denny. 'Out with it,' for he saw that his youthful friend had got an idea and couldn't get it out. You should always listen patiently to the ideas of others, no matter how silly you expect them to be.

'I do wish you wouldn't hurry me so,' said Denny, snapping his fingers anxiously. And we tried to be patient.

'Why shouldn't we *be* them?' Denny said at last.

'He means antiquaries,' said Oswald to the bewildered others. 'But there's nowhere to go and nothing to do when we get there.'

The Dentist (so-called for short, his real name being Denis) got red and white, and drew Oswald aside to the window for a secret discussion. Oswald listened as carefully as he could, but Denny always buzzes so when he whispers.

'Right oh,' he remarked, when the confidings of the Dentist had got so that you could understand what he was driving at. 'Though you're being shy with us now, after all we went through together in the summer, is simply skittles.'

Then he turned to the polite and attentive others and said –

'You remember that day we went to Bexley Heath with Albert's uncle? Well, there was a house, and Albert's uncle said a clever writer lived there, and in more ancient years that chap in history – Sir Thomas What's his name; and Denny thinks he might let us be antiquaries there. It looks a ripping place from the railway.'

It really does. It's a fine big house, and splendid gardens, and a lawn with a sundial, and the tallest trees anywhere about here.

'But what could we *do*?' said Dicky. 'I don't suppose *he'd* give *us* tea,' though such, indeed, had been our hospitable conduct to the antiquaries who came to see Albert's uncle.

'Oh, I don't know,' said Alice. 'We might dress up for it, and wear spectacles, and we could all read papers. It would be lovely – something to fill up the Christmas holidays – the part before the wedding, I mean. Do let's.'

'All right, I don't mind. I suppose it would be improving,' said Dora. 'We should have to read a lot of history. You can settle it. I'm going to show Daisy our bridesmaids' dresses.'

It was, alas! too true. Albert's uncle was to be married but shortly after, and it was partly our faults, though that does not come into this story.

So the two D.'s went to look at the clothes – girls like this – but Alice, who wishes she had never consented to be born a girl, stayed with us, and we had a long and earnest council about it.

'One thing,' said Oswald, 'it can't possibly be wrong – so perhaps it won't be amusing.'

'Oh, Oswald!' said Alice, and she spoke rather like Dora.

'I don't mean what you mean,' said Oswald in lofty scorn. 'What I mean to say is that when a thing is quite sure to be right, it's not so – well – I mean to say there it is, don't you know; and if it might be wrong, and isn't, it's a score to you; and if it might be wrong, and is – as so often happens – well, you know yourself, adventures sometimes turn out wrong that you didn't think were going to, but seldom, or never, the uninteresting kind, and –'

Dicky told Oswald to dry up – which, of course, no one stands from a younger brother, but though Oswald explained this at the time, he felt in his heart that he has sometimes said what he meant with more clearness. When

Oswald and Dicky had finished, we went on and arranged everything.

Every one was to write a paper – and read it.

'If the papers are too long to read while we're there,' said Noël, 'we can read them in the long winter evenings when we are grouped along the household hearthrug. I shall do my paper in poetry – about Agincourt.'

Some of us thought Agincourt wasn't fair, because no one could be sure about any knight who took part in that well-known conflict having lived in the Red House; but Alice got us to agree, because she said it would be precious dull if we all wrote about nothing but Sir Thomas What-doyoucallhim – whose real name in history Oswald said he would find out, and then write his paper on that world-renowned person, who is a household word in all families. Denny said he would write about Charles the First, because they were just doing that part at his school.

'I shall write about what happened in 1066,' said H.O. 'I know that.'

Alice said, 'If I write a paper it will be about Mary Queen of Scots.'

Dora and Daisy came in just as she said this, and it transpired that this ill-fated but good-looking lady was the only one they either of them wanted to write about. So Alice gave it up to them and settled to do Magna Charta, and they could settle something between themselves for the one who would have to give up Mary Queen of Scots in the end. We all agreed that the story of that lamented wearer of pearls and black velvet would not make enough for two papers.

Everything was beautifully arranged, when suddenly H.O. said –

'Supposing he doesn't let us?'

'Who doesn't let us what?'

'The Red House man – read papers at his Red House.'

This was, indeed, what nobody had thought of – and even now we did not think any one could be so lost to proper hospitableness as to say no. Yet none of us liked to write and ask. So we tossed up for it, only Dora had feelings about tossing up on Sunday, so we did it with a hymn-book instead of a penny.

We all won except Noël, who lost, so he said he would do it on Albert's uncle's typewriter, which was on a visit to us at the time, waiting for Mr Remington to fetch it away to mend the 'M'. We think it was broken through Albert's uncle writing 'Margaret' so often, because it is the name of the lady he was doomed to be married by.

The girls had got the letter the Maidstone Antiquarian Society and Field Clubs Secretary had sent to Albert's uncle – H.O. said they kept it for a momentum of the day – and we altered the dates and names in blue chalk and put in a piece about might we skate on the moat, and gave it to Noël, who had already begun to make up his poetry about Agincourt, and so had to be shaken before he would attend. And that evening, when Father and our Indian uncle and Albert's uncle were seeing the others on the way to Forest Hill, Noël's poetry and pencil were taken away from him and he was shut up in Father's room with the Remington typewriter, which we had never been forbidden to touch. And I don't think he hurt it much, except quite at the beginning, when he jammed the 'S' and the 'J' and the thing that means per cent so that they stuck – and Dicky soon put that right with a screwdriver.

He did not get on very well, but kept on writing MOR7E HOAS5 or MORD6M HOVCE on new pieces of paper and then beginning again, till the floor was strewn with his remains; so we left him at it, and went and played Celebrated Painters – a game even Dora cannot say anything about on Sunday, considering the Bible kind of pictures most of them painted. And much later, the library door having banged once and the front door twice, Noël came in and said he had posted it, and already he was deep in poetry again, and had to be roused when requisite for bed.

It was not till next day that he owned that the typewriter had been a fiend in disguise, and that the letter had come out so odd that he could hardly read it himself.

'The hateful engine of destruction wouldn't answer to the bit in the least,' he said, 'and I'd used nearly a wastepaper basket of Father's best paper, and I thought he might come in and say something, so I just finished it as well as I could, and I corrected it with the blue chalk – because you'd bagged that B.B. of mine – and I didn't notice what name I'd signed till after I'd licked the stamp.'

The hearts of his kind brothers and sisters sank low. But they kept them up as well as they could, and said –

'What name *did* you sign?'

And Noël said, 'Why, Edward Turnbull, of course – like at the end of the real letter. You never crossed it out like you did his address.'

'No,' said Oswald witheringly. 'You see, I did think, whatever else you didn't know, I did think you knew your own silly name.'

Then Alice said Oswald was unkind, though you see he was not, and she kissed Noël and said she and he would take turns to watch for the postman, so as to get the answer (which of course would be subscribed on the envelope with the name of Turnbull instead of Bastable) before the servant could tell the postman that the name was a stranger to her.

And next evening it came, and it was very polite and grown-up – and said we should be welcome, and that we might read our papers and skate on the moat. The Red House has a moat, like the Moat House in the country, but not so wild and dangerous. Only we never skated on it because the frost gave out the minute we had got leave to.

Such is life, as the sparks fly upwards. (The last above is called a moral reflection.)

So now, having got leave from Mr Red House (I won't give his name because he is a writer of worldly fame and he might not like it), we set about writing our papers. It was not bad fun, only rather difficult because Dora said she never knew which Encyclo. volume she might be wanting, as she was using Edinburgh, Mary, Scotland, Bothwell, Holywell, and France, and many others, and Oswald never knew which he might want, owing to his not being able exactly to remember the distinguished and deathless other appellation of Sir Thomas Thingummy, who had lived in the Red House.

Noël was up to the ears in Agincourt, yet that made but little difference to our destiny. He is always plunged in poetry of one sort or another, and if it hadn't been that, it would have been something else. This, at least, we insisted on having kept a secret, so he could not read it to us.

H.O. got very inky the first half-holiday, and then he got some sealing-wax and a big envelope from Father, and put something in and fastened it up, and said he had done his.

Dicky would not tell us what his paper was going to be about, but he said it would not be like ours, and he let H.O. help him by looking on while he invented more patent screws for ships.

The spectacles were difficult. We got three pairs of the uncle's, and one that had belonged to the housekeeper's grandfather, but nine pairs were needed, because Albert-next-door mouched in one half-holiday and wanted to join, and said if we'd let him he'd write a paper on the Constitutions of Clarendon, and we thought he couldn't do it, so we let him. And then, after all, he did.

So at last Alice went down to Bennett's in the village, that we are such good customers of, because when our watches stop we take them there, and he lent us a lot of empty frames on the instinctive understanding that we would pay for them if we broke them or let them get rusty.

And so all was ready. And the fatal day approached; and it was the holidays. For us, that is, but not for Father, for his business never seems to rest by day and night, except at Christmas and times like that. So we did not need to ask him if we might go. Oswald thought it would be more amusing for Father if we told it all to him in the form of an entertaining anecdote, afterwards.

Denny and Daisy and Albert came to spend the day.

We told Mrs Blake Mr Red House had asked us, and she let us, and she let the girls put on their second-best things, which are coats with capes and red Tam-o'shanters. These capacious coats are very good for playing highwaymen in.

We made ourselves quite clean and tidy. At the very last we found that H.O. had been making marks on his face with burnt matches, to imitate wrinkles, but really it only imitated dirt, so we made him wash it off. Then he wanted to paint himself red like a clown, but we had decided that the spectacles were to be our only disguise, and even those were not to be assumed till Oswald gave the word.

No casuist observer could have thought that the nine apparently light-headed and careless party who now wended their way to Blackheath Station, looking as if they were not up to anything in particular, were really an Antiquarian Society of the deepest dye. We got an empty carriage to ourselves, and halfway between Blackheath and the other station Oswald gave the word, and we all put on the spectacles. We had our antiquarian papers of lore and researched history in exercise-books, rolled up and tied with string.

The stationmaster and porter, of each of which the station boasted but one specimen, looked respectfully at us as we got out of the train, and we went straight out of the station, under the railway arch, and down to the green gate of the Red House. It has a lodge, but there is no one in it. We peeped in at the window, and there was nothing in the room but an old beehive and a broken leather strap.

We waited in the front for a bit, so that Mr Red House could come out and welcome us like Albert's uncle did the other antiquaries, but no one came, so we went round the garden. It was very brown and wet, but full of things you didn't see every day. Furze summer-houses, for instance, and a red wall all round it, with holes in it that you might have walled heretics up in in the olden times. Some of the holes were quite big enough to have taken a very small heretic. There was a broken swing, a fish-pond – but we were on business, and Oswald insisted on reading the papers.

He said, 'Let's go to the sundial. It looks dryer there, my feet are like ice-houses.'

It was dryer because there was a soaking wet green lawn round it, and round that a sloping path made of little squares of red and white marble. This was quite waterless, and the sun shone on it, so that it was warm to the hands, though not to the feet, because of boots. Oswald called on Albert to read first. Albert is not a clever boy. He is not one of us, and Oswald wanted to get over the Constitutions. For Albert is hardly ever amusing, even in fun, and when he tries to show off it is sometimes hard to bear. He read –

'THE CONSTITUTIONS OF CLARENDON.

'Clarendon (sometimes called Clarence) had only one consti-tution. It must have been a very bad one, because he was killed by a butt of Malmsey. If he had had more constitutions or better ones he would have lived to be very old. This is a warning to every-body.'

To this day none of us know how he could, and whether his uncle helped him.

We clapped, of course, but not with our hearts, which

were hissing inside us, and then Oswald began to read his paper. He had not had a chance to ask Albert's uncle what the other name of the world-famous Sir Thomas was, so he had to put him in as Sir Thomas Blank, and make it up by being very strong on scenes that could be better imagined than described, and, as we knew that the garden was five hundred years old, of course he could bring in any eventful things since the year 1400.

He was just reading the part about the sundial, which he had noticed from the train when we went to Bexley Heath. It was rather a nice piece, I think.

'Most likely this sundial told the time when Charles the First was beheaded, and recorded the death-devouring progress of the Great Plague and the Fire of London. There is no doubt that the sun often shone even in these devastating occasions, so that we may picture Sir Thomas Blank telling the time here and remarking – O crikey!'

These last words are what Oswald himself remarked. Of course a person in history would never have said them.

The reader of the paper had suddenly heard a fierce, woodeny sound, like giant singlesticks, terrifyingly close behind him, and looking hastily round, he saw a most angry lady, in a bright blue dress with fur on it, like a picture, and very large wooden shoes, which had made the singlestick noise. Her eyes were very fierce, and her mouth tight shut. She did not look hideous, but more like an avenging sprite or angel, though of course we knew she was only mortal, so we took off our caps. A gentleman also bounded towards us over some vegetables, and acted as reserve support to the lady.

Her voice when she told us we were trespassing and it was a private garden was not so furious as Oswald had expected from her face, but it *was* angry. H.O. at once said it wasn't her garden, was it? But, of course, we could see it *was*, because of her not having any hat or jacket or gloves, and wearing those wooden shoes to keep her feet dry, which no one would do in the street.

So then Oswald said we had leave, and showed her Mr Red House's letter.

'But that was written to Mr Turnbull,' said she, 'and how did *you* get it?'

Then Mr Red House wearily begged us to explain, so Oswald did, in that clear, straightforward way some people think he has, and that no one can suspect for an instant. And he ended by saying how far from comfortable it would be to have Mr Turnbull coming with his thin mouth and his tight legs, and that we were Bastables, and much nicer than the tight-legged one, whatever she might think.

And she listened, and then she quite suddenly gave a most jolly grin and asked us to go on reading our papers. It was plain that all disagreeableness was at an end, and, to show this even to the stupidest, she instantly asked us to lunch. Before we could politely accept H.O. shoved his oar in as usual and said *he* would stop no matter how little there was for lunch because he liked her very much.

So she laughed, and Mr Red House laughed, and she said they wouldn't interfere with the papers, and they went away and left us.

Of course Oswald and Dicky insisted on going on with the papers; though the girls wanted to talk about Mrs Red House, and how nice she was, and the way her dress was made. Oswald finished his paper, but later he was sorry he had been in such a hurry, because after a bit Mrs Red House came out, and said she wanted to play too. She pretended to be a very ancient antiquary, and was most jolly, so that the others read their papers to her, and Oswald knows she would have liked his paper best, because it *was* the best, though I say it.

Dicky's turned out to be all about the patent screw, and

how Nelson would not have been killed if his ship had been built with one.

Daisy's paper was about Lady Jane Grey, and hers and Dora's were exactly alike, the dullest by far, because they had got theirs out of books.

Alice had not written hers because she had been helping Noël to copy his.

Denny's was about King Charles, and he was very grown-up and fervent about this ill-fated monarch and white roses.

Mrs Red House took us into the summer-houses, where it was warmer, and such is the wonderful architecture of the Red House gardens that there was a fresh summer-house for each paper, except Noël's and H.O.'s, which were read in the stable. There were no horses there.

Noël's was very long, and it began –

> This is the story of Agincourt.
> If you don't know it you jolly well ought.
> It was a famous battle fair,
> And all your ancestors fought there
> That is if you come of a family old.
> The Bastables do; they were always very bold.
> > And at Agincourt
> > > They fought
> > As they ought;
> > So we have been taught.

And so on and so on, till some of us wondered why poetry was ever invented. But Mrs Red House said she liked it awfully, so Noël said –

'You may have it to keep. I've got another one of it at home.'

'I'll put it next my heart, Noël,' she said. And she did, under the blue stuff and fur.

H.O.'s was last, but when we let him read it he wouldn't,

so Dora opened his envelope and it was thick inside with blotting-paper, and in the middle there was a page with

1066 WILLIAM THE CONQUEROR,

and nothing else.

'Well,' he said, 'I said I'd write all I knew about 1066, and that's it. I can't write more than I know, can I?' The girls said he couldn't, but Oswald thought he might have tried.

'It wasn't worth blacking your face all over just for that,' he said. But Mrs Red House laughed very much and said it was a lovely paper, and told *her* all she wanted to know about 1066.

Then we went into the garden again and ran races, and Mrs Red House held all our spectacles for us and cheered us on. She said she was the Patent Automatic Cheering Winning-post. We do like her.

Lunch was the glorious end of the Morden House Antiquarian Society and Field Club's Field Day. But after lunch was the beginning of a real adventure such as real antiquarians hardly ever get. This will be unrolled later. I will finish with some French out of a newspaper. Albert's uncle told it me, so I know it is right. Any of your own grown-ups will tell you what it means.

Au prochain numéro je vous promets des émotions.

P.S. – In case your grown-ups can't be bothered, '*émotions*' means sensation, I believe.

THE INTREPID EXPLORER AND
HIS LIEUTENANT

WE had spectacles to play antiquaries in, and the rims were vaselined to prevent rust, and it came off on our faces with other kinds of dirt, and when the antiquary game was over, Mrs Red House helped us to wash it off with all the thoroughness of aunts, and far more gentleness.

Then, clean and with our hairs brushed, we were led from the bath-room to the banqueting hall or dining-room.

It is a very beautiful house. The girls thought it was bare, but Oswald likes bareness because it leaves more room for games. All the furniture was of agreeable shapes and colours, and so were all the things on the table – glasses and dishes and everything. Oswald politely said how nice everything was.

The lunch was a blissful dream of perfect A.1.-ness. Tongue, and nuts, and apples, and oranges, and candied fruits, and ginger-wine and tiny glasses that Noël said were fairy goblets. Everybody drank everybody else's health – and Noël told Mrs Red House just how lovely she was, and he would have paper and pencil and write her a poem for her very own. I will not put it in here, because Mr Red House is an author himself, and he might want to use it in some of his books. And the writer of these pages has been taught to think of others, and besides I expect you are jolly well sick of Noël's poetry.

There was no restrainingness about that lunch. As far as a married lady can possibly be a regular brick, Mrs Red House is one. And Mr Red House is not half bad, and knows how to talk about interesting things like sieges, and cricket, and foreign postage stamps.

Even poets think of things sometimes, and it was Noël who said directly he had finished his poetry,

'Have you got a secret staircase? And have you explored your house properly?'

'Yes – we have,' said that well-behaved and unusual lady – Mrs Red House, 'but *you* haven't. You may if you like. Go anywhere,' she added with the unexpected magnificence of a really noble heart. 'Look at everything – only don't make hay. Off with you!' or words to that effect.

And the whole of us, with proper thanks, offed with us instantly, in case she should change her mind.

I will not describe the Red House to you – because perhaps you do not care about a house having three staircases and more cupboards and odd corners than we'd ever seen before, and great attics with beams, and enormous drawers on rollers, let into the wall – and half the rooms not furnished, and those that were all with old-looking, interesting furniture. There was something about that furniture that even the present author can't describe – as though any of it might have secret drawers or panels – even the chairs. It was all beautiful, and mysterious in the deepest degree.

When we had been all over the house several times, we thought about the cellars. There was only one servant in the kitchen (so we saw Mr and Mrs Red House must be poor but honest, like we used to be), and we said to her –

'How do you do? We've got leave to go wherever we like, and please where are the cellars, and may we go in?'

She was quite nice, though she seemed to think there was an awful lot of us. People often think this. She said:

'Lor, love a duck – yes, I suppose so,' in not ungentle tones, and showed us.

I don't think we should ever have found the way from the

house into the cellar by ourselves. There was a wide shelf in the scullery with a row of gentlemanly boots on it that had been cleaned, and on the floor in front a piece of wood. The general servant – for such indeed she proved to be – lifted up the wood and opened a little door under the shelf. And there was the beginning of steps, and the entrance to them was half trap-door, and half the upright kind – a thing none of us had seen before.

She gave us a candle-end, and we pressed forward to the dark unknown. The stair was of stone, arched overhead like churches – and it twisted most unlike other cellar stairs. And when we got down it was all arched like vaults, very cobwebby.

'Just the place for crimes,' said Dicky. There was a beer cellar, and a wine cellar with bins, and a keeping cellar with hooks in the ceiling and stone shelves – just right for venison pasties and haunches of the same swift animal.

Then we opened a door and there was a cellar with a well in it.

'To throw bodies down, no doubt,' Oswald explained.

They were cellars full of glory, and passages leading from one to the other like the Inquisition, and I wish ours at home were like them.

There was a pile of beer barrels in the largest cellar, and it was H.O. who said, 'Why not play "King of the Castle"?'

So we did. We had a most refreshing game. It was exactly like Denny to be the one who slipped down behind the barrels, and did not break a single one of all his legs or arms.

'No,' he cried, in answer to our anxious inquiries. 'I'm not hurt a bit, but the wall here feels soft – at least not soft – but it doesn't scratch your nails like stone does, so perhaps it's the door of a secret dungeon or something like that.'

'Good old Dentist!' replied Oswald, who always likes Denny to have ideas of his own, because it was us who taught him the folly of white-mousishness.

'It might be,' he went on, 'but these barrels are as heavy as lead, and much more awkward to collar hold of.'

'Couldn't we get in some other way?' Alice said. 'There ought to be a subterranean passage. I expect there is if we only knew.'

Oswald has an enormous geographical bump in his head. He said –

'Look here! That far cellar, where the wall doesn't go quite up to the roof – that space we made out was under the dining-room – I could creep under there. I believe it leads into behind this door.'

'Get me out! Oh do, do get me out, and let me come!' shouted the barrel-imprisoned Dentist from the unseen regions near the door.

So we got him out by Oswald lying flat on his front on the top barrel, and the Dentist clawed himself up by Oswald's hands while the others kept hold of the boots of the representative of the house of Bastable, which, of course, Oswald is, whenever Father is not there.

'Come on,' cried Oswald, when Denny was at last able to appear, very cobwebby and black. 'Give us what's left of the matches!'

The others agreed to stand by the barrels and answer our knocking on the door if we ever got there.

'But I daresay we shall perish on the way,' said Oswald hopefully.

So we started. The other cellar was easily found by the ingenious and geography-bump-headed Oswald. It opened straight on to the moat, and we think it was a boathouse in middle-aged times.

Denny made a back for Oswald, who led the way, and then he turned round and hauled up his inexperienced, but rapidly improving, follower on to the top of the wall that did not go quite up to the roof.

'It is like coal mines,' he said, beginning to crawl on hands and knees over what felt like very prickly beach, 'only we've no picks or shovels.'

'And no Sir Humphry Davy safety lamps,' said Denny in sadness.

'They wouldn't be any good,' said Oswald; 'they're only to protect the hard-working mining men against fire-damp and choke-damp. And there's none of those kinds here.'

'No,' said Denny, 'the damp here is only just the common kind.'

'Well, then,' said Oswald, and they crawled a bit further still on their furtive and unassuming stomachs.

'This is a very glorious adventure. It is, isn't it?' inquired the Dentist in breathlessness, when the young stomachs of the young explorers had bitten the dust for some yards further.

'Yes,' said Oswald, encouraging the boy, 'and it's *your* find, too,' he added, with admirable fairness and justice, unusual in one so young. 'I only hope we shan't find a mouldering skeleton buried alive behind that door when we get to it. Come on. What are you stopping for now?' he added kindly.

'It's – it's only cobwebs in my throat,' Denny remarked, and he came on, though slower than before.

Oswald, with his customary intrepid caution, was leading the way, and he paused every now and then to strike a match because it was pitch dark, and at any moment the courageous leader might have tumbled into a well or a dungeon, or knocked his dauntless nose against something in the dark.

'It's all right for you,' he said to Denny, when he had happened to kick his follower in the eye. 'You've nothing to fear except my boots, and whatever they do is accidental, and so it doesn't count, but *I* may be going straight into some trap that has been yawning for me for countless ages.'

'I won't come on so fast, thank you,' said the Dentist. 'I don't think you've kicked my eye out yet.'

So they went on and on, crampedly crawling on what I have mentioned before, and at last Oswald did not strike the next match carefully enough, and with the suddenness of a falling star his hands, which, with his knees, he was crawling on, went over the edge into infinite space, and his chest alone, catching sharply on the edge of the precipice, saved him from being hurled to the bottom of it.

'Halt!' he cried, as soon as he had any breath again. But, alas! it was too late! The Dentist's nose had been too rapid, and had caught up the boot-heel of the daring leader. This was very annoying to Oswald, and was not in the least his fault.

'Do keep your nose off my boots half a sec.,' he remarked, but not crossly. 'I'll strike a match.'

And he did, and by its weird and unscrutatious light looked down into the precipice.

Its bottom transpired to be not much more than six feet below, so Oswald turned the other end of himself first, hung by his hands, and dropped with fearless promptness, uninjured, in another cellar. He then helped Denny down. The cornery thing Denny happened to fall on could not have hurt him so much as he said.

The light of the torch, I mean match, now revealed to the two bold and youthful youths another cellar, with *things* in it – very dirty indeed, but of thrilling interest and unusual shapes, but the match went out before we could see exactly what the things were.

The next match was the last but one, but Oswald was undismayed, whatever Denny may have been. He lighted it and looked hastily round. There was a door.

'Bang on that door – over there, silly!' he cried, in cheering accents, to his trusty lieutenant; 'behind that thing that looks like a *chevaux de frize*.'

Denny had never been to Woolwich, and while Oswald was explaining what a *chevaux de frize* is, the match burnt his fingers almost to the bone, and he had to feel his way to the door and hammer on it himself.

The blows of the others from the other side were deafening.

All was saved.

It was the right door.

'Go and ask for candles and matches,' shouted the brave Oswald. 'Tell them there are all sorts of things in here – a *chevaux de frize* of chair-legs, and –'

'A shovel of *what*?' asked Dicky's voice hollowly from the other side of the door.

'Freeze,' shouted Denny. 'I don't know what it means, but do get a candle and make them unbarricade the door. I don't want to go back the way we came.' He said something about Oswald's boots that he was sorry for afterwards, so I will not repeat it, and I don't think the others heard, because of the noise the barrels made while they were being climbed over.

This noise, however, was like balmy zephyrs compared to the noise the barrels insisted on making when Dicky had collected some grown-ups and the barrels were being rolled away. During this thunder-like interval Denny and Oswald were all the time in the pitch dark. They had lighted their last match, and by its flickering gleam we saw a long, large mangle.

'It's like a double coffin,' said Oswald, as the match went out. 'You can take my arm if you like, Dentist.'

The Dentist did – and then afterwards he said he only did it because he thought Oswald was frightened of the dark.

'It's only for a little while,' said Oswald in the pauses of the barrel-thunder, 'and I once read about two brothers confined for life in a cage so constructed that the unfortunate prisoners could neither sit, lie, nor stand in comfort. We can do all those things.'

'Yes,' said Denny; 'but I'd rather keep on standing if it's the same to you, Oswald. I don't like spiders – not much, that is.'

'You are right,' said Oswald with affable gentleness; 'and there might be toads perhaps in a vault like this – or serpents guarding the treasure like in the Cold Lairs. But of course they couldn't have cobras in England. They'd have to put up with vipers, I suppose.'

Denny shivered, and Oswald could feel him stand first on one leg and then on the other.

'I wish I could stand on neither of my legs for a bit,' he said, but Oswald answered firmly that this could not be.

And then the door opened with a crash crash, and we saw lights and faces through it, and something fell from the top of the door that Oswald really did think for one awful instant was a hideous mass of writhing serpents put there to guard the entrance.

'Like a sort of live booby-trap,' he explained; 'just the sort of thing a magician or a witch would have thought of doing.'

But it was only dust and cobwebs – a thick, damp mat of them.

Then the others surged in, in light-hearted misunderstanding of the perils Oswald had led Denny into – I mean through, with Mr Red House and another gentleman, and loud voices and candles that dripped all over everybody's hands, as well as their clothes, and the solitary confinement of the gallant Oswald was at an end. Denny's solitary confinement was at an end, too – and he was now able to stand on both legs and to let go the arm of his leader who was so full of fortitude.

'This *is* a find,' said the pleased voice of Mr Red House. 'Do you know, we've been in this house six whole months and a bit, and *we* never thought of there being a door here.'

'Perhaps you don't often play "King of the Castle",' said Dora politely; 'it *is* rather a rough game, I always think.'

'Well, curiously enough, we never have,' said Mr Red House, beginning to lift out the chairs, in which avocation we all helped, of course.

'Nansen is nothing to you! You ought to have a medal for daring explorations,' said the other gentleman, but nobody gave us one, and, of course, we did not want any reward for doing our duty, however tight and cobwebby.

The cellars proved to be well stocked with spiders and old furniture, but no toads or snakes, which few, if any, regretted. Snakes are outcasts from human affection. Oswald pities them, of course.

There was a great lumpish thing in four parts that Mr Red House said was a press, and a ripping settle – besides the chairs, and some carved wood that Mr Red House and his friend made out to be part of an old four-post bed. There was also a wooden thing like a box with another box on it at one end, and H.O. said –

'You could make a ripping rabbit-hutch out of that.'

Oswald thought so himself. But Mr Red House said he had other uses for it, and would bring it up later.

It took us all that was left of the afternoon to get the things up the stairs into the kitchen. It was hard work, but we know all about the dignity of labour. The general hated the things we had so enterprisingly discovered. I suppose she knew who would have to clean them, but Mrs Red House was awfully pleased and said we were dears.

We were not very clean dears by the time our work was done, and when the other gentleman said, 'Won't you all take a dish of tea under my humble roof?' the words 'Like this?' were formed by more than one youthful voice.

'Well, if you would be happier in a partially cleansed state?' said Mr Red House. And Mrs Red House, who is my idea of a feudal lady in a castle, said, 'Oh, come along, let's go and partially clean ourselves. I'm dirtier than anybody, though I haven't explored a bit. I've often noticed that the more you admire things the more they come off on you!'

So we all washed as much as we cared to, and went to tea at the gentleman's house, which was only a cottage, but very beautiful. He had been a war correspondent, and he knew a great many things, besides having books and books of pictures.

It was a splendid party.

We thanked Mrs R.H. and everybody when it was time to go, and she kissed the girls and the little boys, and then she put her head on one side and looked at Oswald and said, 'I suppose you're too old?'

Oswald did not like to say he was not. If kissed at all he would prefer it being for some other reason than his being not too old for it. So he did not know what to say. But Noël chipped in with –

'You'll never be too old for it,' to Mrs Red House – which seemed to Oswald most silly and unmeaning, because she was already much too old to be kissed by people unless she chose to begin it. But every one seemed to think Noël had said something clever. And Oswald felt like a young ass. But Mrs R. H. looked at him so kindly and held out her hand so queenily that, before he knew he meant to, he had kissed it like you do the Queen's. Then, of course, Denny and Dicky went and did the same. Oswald wishes that the word 'kiss' might never be spoken again in this world. Not that he minded kissing Mrs Red House's hand in the least, especially as she seemed to think it was nice of him to – but the whole thing is such contemptible piffle.

We were seen home by the gentleman who wasn't Mr

Red House, and he stood a glorious cab with a white horse who had a rolling eye, from Blackheath Station, and so ended one of the most adventuring times we ever got out of a play-beginning.

The *time* ended as the author has pointed out, but not its resultingness. Thus we ever find it in life – the most unharmful things, thoroughly approved even by grown-ups, but too often lead to something quite different, and that no one can possibly approve of, not even yourself when you come to think it over afterwards, like Noël and H.O. had to.

It was but natural that the hearts of the young explorers should have dwelt fondly on everything underground, even drains, which was what made us read a book by Mr Hugo, all the next day. It is called 'The Miserables', in French, and the man in it, who is a splendid hero, though a convict and a robber and various other professions, escapes into a drain with great rats in it, and is miraculously restored to the light of day, unharmed by the kindly rodents. (N.B. – Rodents mean rats.)

When we had finished all the part about drains it was nearly dinner-time, and Noël said quite suddenly in the middle of a bite of mutton –

'The Red House isn't nearly so red as ours is outside. Why should the cellars be so much cellarier? Shut up H.O.!' For H.O. was trying to speak.

Dora explained to him how we don't all have exactly the same blessings, but he didn't seem to see it.

'It doesn't seem like the way things happen in books,' he said. 'In Walter Scott it wouldn't be like that, nor yet in Anthony Hope. I should think the rule would be the redder the cellarier. If I was putting it into poetry I should make our cellars have something much wonderfuller in them than just wooden things. H.O., if you don't shut up I'll never let you be in anything again.'

'There's that door you go down steps to,' said Dicky; 'we've never been in there. If Dora and I weren't going with Miss Blake to be fitted for boots we might try that.'

'That's just what I was coming to. (Stow it, H.O.!) I felt just like cellars to-day, while you other chaps were washing your hands for din. – and it was very cold; but I made H.O. feel the same, and we went down, and – that door *isn't shut now*.'

The intelligible reader may easily guess that we finished our dinner as quickly as we could, and we put on our outers, sympathizing with Dicky and Dora, who, owing to boots, were out of it, and we went into the garden. There are five steps down to that door. They were red brick when they began, but now they are green with age and mysteriousness and not being walked on. And at the bottom of them the door was, as Noël said, not fastened. We went in.

'It isn't beery, winey cellars at all,' Alice said; 'it's more like a robber's store-house. Look there.'

We had got to the inner cellar, and there were heaps of carrots and other vegetables.

'Halt, my men!' cried Oswald, 'advance not an inch further! The bandits may lurk not a yard from you!'

'Suppose they jump out on us?' said H.O.

'They will not rashly leap into the light,' said the discerning Oswald. And he went to fetch a new dark-lantern of his that he had not had any chance of really using before. But some one had taken Oswald's secret matches, and then the beastly lantern wouldn't light for ever so long. But he thought it didn't matter his being rather a long time gone, because the others could pass the time in wondering whether anything would jump out on them, and if so, what and when.

So when he got back to the red steps and the open door and flashed his glorious bull's-eye round it was rather an annoying thing for there not to be a single other eye for it to flash into. Every one had vanished.

'Hallo!' cried Oswald, and if his gallant voice trembled he is not ashamed of it, because he knows about wells in cellars, and, for an instant, even he did not know what had happened.

But an answering hullo came from beyond, and he hastened after the others.

'Look out,' said Alice; 'don't tumble over that heap of bones.'

Oswald did look out – of course, he would not wish to walk on any one's bones. But he did not jump back with a scream, whatever Noël may say when he is in a temper.

The heap really did look very like bones, partly covered with earth. Oswald was glad to learn that they were only parsnips.

'We waited as long as we could,' said Alice, 'but we thought perhaps you'd been collared for some little thing you'd forgotten all about doing, and wouldn't be able to come back, but we found Noël had, fortunately, got your matches. I'm so glad you weren't collared, Oswald dear.'

Some boys would have let Noël know about the matches, but Oswald didn't. The heaps of carrots and turnips and parsnips and things were not very interesting when you knew that they were not bleeding warriors' or pilgrims' bones, and it was too cold to pretend for long with any comfort to the young Pretenders. So Oswald said –

'Let's go out on the Heath and play something warm. You can't warm yourself with matches, even if they're not your own.'

That was all he said. A great hero would not stoop to argue about matches.

And Alice said, 'All right', and she and Oswald went out and played pretending golf with some walking-sticks of

Father's. But Noël and H.O. preferred to sit stuffily over the common-room fire. So that Oswald and Alice, as well as Dora and Dicky, who were being measured for boots, were entirely out of the rest of what happened, and the author can only imagine the events that now occurred.

When Noël and H.O. had roasted their legs by the fire till they were so hot that their stockings quite hurt them, one of them must have said to the other – I never knew which:

'Let's go and have another look at that cellar.'

The other – whoever it was – foolishly consented. So they went, and they took Oswald's dark-lantern in his absence and without his leave.

They found a hitherto unnoticed door behind the other one, and Noël says he said, 'We'd better not go in.' H.O. says he said so too. But any way, they *did* go in.

They found themselves in a small vaulted place that we found out afterwards had been used for mushrooms. But it was long since any fair bud of a mushroom had blossomed in that dark retreat. The place had been cleaned and new shelves put up, and when Noël and H.O. saw what was on these shelves the author is sure they turned pale, though they say not.

For what they saw was coils, and pots, and wires; and one of them said, in a voice that must have trembled –

'It is dynamite, I am certain of it; what shall we do?'

I am certain the other said, 'This is to blow up Father because he took part in the Lewisham Election, and his side won.'

The reply no doubt was, 'There is no time for delay; we must act. We must cut the fuse – all the fuses; there are dozens.'

Oswald thinks it was not half bad business, those two kids – for Noël is little more than one, owing to his poetry and his bronchitis – standing in the abode of dynamite and

not screeching, or running off to tell Miss Blake, or the
servants, or any one – but just doing *the right thing* without
any fuss.

I need hardly say it did not prove to be the right thing –
but they thought it was. And Oswald cannot think that you
are really doing wrong if you really think you are doing
right. I hope you will understand this.

I believe the kids tried cutting the fuses with Dick's
pocket-knife that was in the pocket of his other clothes. But
the fuses would not – no matter how little you trembled
when you touched them.

But at last, with scissors and the gas pliers, they cut every
fuse. The fuses were long, twisty, wire things covered with
green wool, like blind-cords.

Then Noël and H.O. (and Oswald for one thinks it
showed a goodish bit of pluck, and policemen have been
made heroes for less) got cans and cans of water from the
tap by the greenhouse and poured sluicing showers of the
icy fluid in among the internal machinery of the dynamite
arrangement – for so they believed it to be.

Then, very wet, but feeling that they had saved their
father and the house, they went and changed their clothes.
I think they were a little stuck-up about it, believing it to be
an act unrivalled in devotedness, and they were most
tiresome all the afternoon, talking about their secret, and
not letting us know what it was.

But when Father came home, early, as it happened, those
swollen-headed, but, in Oswald's opinion, quite-to-be-
excused, kiddies learned the terrible truth.

Of course Oswald and Dicky would have known at once;
if Noël and H.O. hadn't been so cocky about not telling us,
we could have exposed the truth to them in all its uninteresting nature.

I hope the reader will now prepare himself for a shock. In
a wild whirl of darkness, and the gas being cut off, and not

being able to get any light, and Father saying all sorts of things, it all came out.

Those coils and jars and wires in that cellar were not an infernal machine at all. It was – I know you will be very much surprised – it was the electric lights and bells that Father had had put in while we were at the Red House the day before.

H.O. and Noël caught it very fully; and Oswald thinks this was one of the few occasions when my father was not as just as he meant to be. My uncle was not just either, but then it is much longer since he was a boy, so we must make excuses for him.

We sent Mrs Red House a Christmas card each. In spite of the trouble that her cellars had lured him into, Noël sent her a home-made one with an endless piece of his everlasting poetry on it, and next May she wrote and asked us to come and see her. *We* try to be just, and we saw that it was not really her fault that Noël and H.O. had cut those electric wires, so we all went; but we did not take Albert Morrison, because he was fortunately away with an aged god-parent of his mother's who writes tracts at Tunbridge Wells.

The garden was all flowery and green, and Mr and Mrs Red House were nice and jolly, and we had a distinguished and first-class time.

But would you believe it? – that boxish thing in the cellar, that H.O. wanted them to make a rabbit-hutch of – well, Mr Red House had cleaned it and mended it, and Mrs Red House took us up to the room where it was, to let us look at it again. And, unbelievable to relate, it turned out to have rockers, and some one in dark, bygone ages seems, for reasons unknown to the present writer, to have wasted no end of carpentry and carving on it, just to make it into a *Cradle*. And what is more, since we were there last Mr and

Mrs Red House had succeeded in obtaining a small but quite alive baby to put in it.

I suppose they thought it was wilful waste to have a cradle and no baby to use it. But it could so easily have been used for something else. It would have made a ripping rabbit-hutch, and babies are far more trouble than rabbits to keep, and not nearly so profitable, I believe.

THE TURK IN CHAINS; OR,
RICHARD'S REVENGE

THE morning dawned in cloudless splendour. The sky was a pale cobalt colour, as in pictures of Swiss scenery. The sun shone brightly, and all the green things in the garden sparkled in the bewitching rays of the monarch of the skies.

The author of this does not like to read much about the weather in books, but he is obliged to put this piece in because it is true; and it is a thing that does not very often happen in the middle of January. In fact, I never remember the weather being at all like that in the winter except on that one day.

Of course we all went into the garden directly after brekker. (PS. – I have said green things: perhaps you think that is a *lapsus lazuli*, or slip of the tongue, and that there are not any green things in the winter. But there are. And not just evergreens either. Wallflowers and pansies and snapdragons and primroses, and lots of things, keep green all the year unless it's too frosty. Live and learn.)

And it was so warm we were able to sit in the summer-house. The birds were singing like mad. Perhaps they thought it was springtime. Or perhaps they always sing when they see the sun, without paying attention to dates.

And now, when all his brothers and sisters were sitting on the rustic seats in the summer-house, the far-sighted Oswald suddenly saw that now was the moment for him to hold that council he had been wanting to hold for some time.

So he stood in the door of the summer-house, in case any

of the others should suddenly remember that they wanted to be in some other place. And he said –

'I say. About that council I want to hold.'

And Dicky replied: 'Well, what about it?'

So then Oswald explained all over again that we had been Treasure Seekers, and we had been Would-be-Goods, and he thought it was time we were something else.

'Being something else makes you think of things,' he said at the end of all the other things he said.

'Yes,' said H.O., yawning, without putting up his hand, which is not manners, and we told him so. 'But *I* can think of things without being other things. Look how I thought about being a clown, and going to Rome.'

'I shouldn't think you would want us to remember *that*,' said Dora. And indeed Father had not been pleased with H.O. about that affair. But Oswald never encourages Dora to nag, so he said patiently –

'Yes, you think of things you'd much better not have thought of. Now my idea is let's each say what sort of a society we shall make ourselves into – like we did when we were Treasure Seekers – about the different ways to look for it, I mean. Let's hold our tongues (no, not with your dirty fingers, H.O., old chap; hold it with your teeth if you must hold it with something) – let's hold our tongues for a bit, and then all say what we've thought of – in ages,' the thoughtful boy added hastily, so that every one should not speak at once when we had done holding our tongues.

So we were all silent, and the birds sang industriously among the leafless trees of our large sunny garden in beautiful Blackheath. (The author is sorry to see he is getting poetical. It shall not happen again, and it *was* an extra fine day, really, and the birds did sing, a fair treat.)

When three long minutes had elapsed themselves by the hands of Oswald's watch, which always keeps perfect time

for three or four days after he has had it mended, he closed
the watch and observed –

'Time! Go ahead, Dora.'

Dora went ahead in the following remarks:

'I've thought as hard as I can, and nothing will come into
my head except –

> *Be good, sweet maid, and let who will be clever.*

Don't you think we might try to find some new ways to be
good in?'

'No, you don't!' 'I bar that!' came at once from the
mouths of Dicky and Oswald.

'You don't come that over us twice,' Dicky added. And
Oswald eloquently said, 'No more Would-be-Goods, thank
you, Dora.'

Dora said, well, she couldn't think of anything else. And
she didn't expect Oswald had thought of anything better.

'Yes, I have,' replied her brother. 'What I think is that we
don't *know* half enough.'

'If you mean extra swat,' said Alice; 'I've more homers
than I care for already, thank you.'

'I do not mean swat,' rejoined the experienced Oswald. 'I
want to know all about real things, not booky things. If you
kids had known about electric bells you wouldn't have –'
Oswald stopped, and then said, 'I won't say any more,
because Father says a gentleman does not support his
arguments with personal illusions to other people's faults
and follies.'

'Faults and follies yourself,' said H.O. The girls restored
peace, and Oswald went on –

'Let us seek to grow wiser, and to teach each other.'

'*I* bar that,' said H.O. 'I don't want Oswald and Dicky
always on to me and call it teaching.'

'We might call the society the Would-be-Wisers,' said
Oswald hastily.

'It's not so dusty,' said Dicky; 'let's go on to the others before we decide.'

'You're next yourself,' said Alice.

'Oh, so I am,' remarked Dicky, trying to look surprised. 'Well, my idea is let's be a sort of Industrious Society of Beavers, and make a solemn vow and covenant to make something every day. We might call it the Would-be-Clevers.'

'It would be the Too-clever-by-half's before we'd done with it,' said Oswald.

And Alice said, 'We couldn't always make things that would be any good, and then we should have to do something that wasn't any good, and that would be rot. Yes, I know it's my turn – H.O., you'll kick the table to pieces if you go on like that. Do, for goodness' sake, keep your feet still. The only thing I can think of is a society called the Would-be-Boys.'

'With you and Dora for members.'

'And Noël – poets aren't boys exactly,' said H.O.

'If you don't shut up you shan't be in it at all,' said Alice, putting her arm round Noël. 'No; I meant us all to be in it – only you boys are not to keep saying we're only girls, and let us do everything the same as you boys do.'

'I don't want to be a boy, thank you,' said Dora, 'not when I see how they behave. H.O., *do* stop sniffing and use your handkerchief. Well, take mine, then.'

It was now Noël's turn to disclose his idea, which proved most awful.

'Let's be Would-be-Poets,' he said, 'and solemnly vow and convenient to write one piece of poetry a day as long as we live.'

Most of us were dumb at the dreadful thought. But Alice said –

'That would never do, Noël dear, because you're the only one of us who's clever enough to do it.'

So Noël's detestable and degrading idea was shelved without Oswald having to say anything that would have made the youthful poet weep.

'I suppose you don't mean me to say what I thought of,' said H.O., 'but I shall. I think you ought all to be in a Would-be-Kind Society, and vow solemn convents and things not to be down on your younger brother.'

We explained to him at once that *he* couldn't be in that, because he hadn't got a younger brother.

'And you may think yourself lucky you haven't,' Dicky added.

The ingenious and felicitous Oswald was just going to begin about the council all over again, when the portable form of our Indian uncle came stoutly stumping down the garden path under the cedars.

'Hi, brigands!' he cried in his cheerful unclish manner. 'Who's on for the Hippodrome this bright day?'

And instantly we all were. Even Oswald – because after all you can have a council any day, but Hippodromes are not like that.

We got ready like the whirlwind of the desert for quickness, and started off with our kind uncle, who has lived so long in India that he is much more warm-hearted than you would think to look at him.

Half-way to the station Dicky remembered his patent screw for working ships with. He had been messing with it in the bath while he was waiting for Oswald to have done plunging cleanly in the basin. And in the desert-whirlwinding he had forgotten to take it out. So now he ran back, because he knew how its cardboardiness would turn to pulp if it was left.

'I'll catch you up,' he cried.

The uncle took the tickets and the train came in and still Dicky had not caught us up.

'Tiresome boy!' said the uncle; 'you don't want to miss

the beginning – eh, what? Ah, here he comes!' The uncle got in, and so did we, but Dicky did not see the uncle's newspaper which Oswald waved, and he went running up and down the train looking for us instead of just getting in anywhere sensibly, as Oswald would have done. When the train began to move he did try to open a carriage door but it stuck, and the train went faster, and just as he got it open a large heavy porter caught him by the collar and pulled him off the train, saying –

'Now, young shaver, no susansides on this 'ere line, if *you* please.'

Dicky hit the porter, but his fury was vain. Next moment the train had passed away, and us in it. Dicky had no money, and the uncle had all the tickets in the pocket of his fur coat.

I am not going to tell you anything about the Hippodrome because the author feels that it was a trifle beastly of us to have enjoyed it as much as we did considering Dicky. We tried not to talk about it before him when we got home, but it was very difficult – especially the elephants.

I suppose he spent an afternoon of bitter thoughts after he had told that porter what he thought of him, which took some time, and the station-master interfered in the end.

When we got home he was all right with us. He had had time to see it was not our faults, whatever he thought at the time.

He refused to talk about it. Only he said –

'I'm going to take it out of that porter. You leave me alone. I shall think of something presently.'

'Revenge is very wrong,' said Dora; but even Alice asked her kindly to dry up. We all felt that it was simply piffle to talk copy-book to one so disappointed as our unfortunate brother.

'It *is* wrong, though,' said Dora.

'Wrong be blowed!' said Dicky, snorting; 'who began it I should like to know! The station's a beastly awkward place to take it out of any one in. I wish I knew where he lived.'

'*I* know *that*,' said Noël. 'I've known it a long time – before Christmas, when we were going to the Moat House.'

'Well, what is it, then?' asked Dicky savagely.

'Don't bite his head off,' remarked Alice. 'Tell us about it, Noël. How do you know?'

'It was when you were weighing yourselves on the weighing machine. I didn't because my weight isn't worth being weighed for. And there was a heap of hampers and turkeys and hares and things, and there was a label on a turkey and brown-paper parcel; and that porter that you hate so said to the other porter –'

'Oh, hurry up, do!' said Dicky.

'I won't tell you at all if you bully me,' said Noël, and Alice had to coax him before he would go on.

'Well, he looked at the label and said, "Little mistake here, Bill – wrong address; ought to be 3, Abel Place, eh?"

'And the other one looked, and he said, "Yes; it's got your name right enough. Fine turkey, too, and his chains in the parcel. Pity they ain't more careful about addressing things, eh?" So when they had done laughing about it I looked at the label and it said, "James Johnson, 8, Granville Park." So I knew it was 3, Abel Place, he lived at, and his name was James Johnson.'

'Good old Sherlock Holmes!' said Oswald.

'You won't really *hurt* him,' said Noël, 'will you? Not Corsican revenge with knives, or poisoned bowls? I wouldn't do more than a good booby-trap, if I was you.'

When Noël said the word 'booby-trap', we all saw a strange, happy look come over Dicky's face. It is called a far-away look, I believe, and you can see it in the picture of a woman cuddling a photograph-album with her hair down, that is in all the shops, and they call it 'The Soul's Awakening'.

Directly Dicky's soul had finished waking up he shut his teeth together with a click. Then he said, 'I've got it.'

Of course we all knew that.

'Any one who thinks revenge is wrong is asked to leave *now*.'

Dora said he was very unkind, and did he really want to turn her out?

'There's a jolly good fire in Father's study,' he said. 'No, I'm not waxy with you, but I'm going to have my revenge, and I don't want you to do anything you thought wrong. You'd only make no end of a fuss afterwards.'

'Well, it *is* wrong, so I'll go,' said Dora. 'Don't say I didn't warn you, that's all!'

And she went.

Then Dicky said, 'Now, any more conscious objectors?'

And when no one replied he went on: 'It was you saying "Booby-trap" gave me the idea. His name's James Johnson, is it? And he said the things were addressed wrong, did he? Well, *I'll* send him a Turkey-and-chains.'

'A Turk in chains,' said Noël, growing owley-eyed at the thought – 'a *live* Turk – or – no, not a dead one, Dicky?'

'The Turk I'm going to send won't be a live one nor yet a dead one.'

'How horrible! *Half* dead. That's worse than anything,' and Noël became so green in the face that Alice told Dicky to stop playing the goat, and tell us what his idea really was.

'Don't you see *yet*?' he cried; '*I* saw it directly.'

'I daresay,' said Oswald; 'it's easy to see your own idea. Drive ahead.'

'Well, I'm going to get a hamper and pack it full of parcels and put a list of them on the top – beginning Turk-and-chains, and send it to Mister James Johnson, and when he opens the parcels there'll be nothing inside.'

'There must be something, you know,' said H.O., 'or the parcels won't be any shape except flatness.'

'Oh, there'll be *something* right enough,' was the bitter reply of the one who had not been to the Hippodrome, 'but it won't be the sort of something he'll expect it to be. Let's do it now. I'll get a hamper.'

He got a big one out of the cellar and four empty bottles with their straw cases. We filled the bottles with black ink and water, and red ink and water, and soapy water, and water plain. And we put them down on the list –

1 bottle of port wine.
1 bottle of sherry wine.
1 bottle of sparkling champagne.
1 bottle of rum.

The rest of the things we put on the list were –

1 turkey-and-chains.
2 pounds of chains.
1 plum pudding.
4 pounds of mince pies.
2 pounds of almonds and raisins.
1 box of figs.
1 bottle of French plums.
1 large cake.

And we made up parcels to look outside as if their inside was full of the delicious attributes described in the list. It was rather difficult to get anything the shape of a turkey but with coals and crushed newspapers and firewood we did it, and when it was done up with lots of string and the paper artfully squeezed tight to the firewood to look like the Turk's legs it really was almost lifelike in its deceivingness. The chains, or sausages, we did with dusters – and not clean ones – rolled tight, and the paper moulded gently to their forms. The plum-pudding was a newspaper ball. The mince-pies were newspapers too, and so were the almonds and raisins. The box of figs was a real fig-box with cinders and ashes in it damped to keep them from rattling about. The French-plum bottle was real too. It had newspaper soaked in ink in it, and the cake was half a muff-box of Dora's done up very carefully and put at the bottom of the hamper. Inside the muff-box we put a paper with –

'Revenge is not wrong when the other people begin. It was you began, and now you are jolly well served out.'

We packed all the bottles and parcels into the hamper, and put the list on the very top, pinned to the paper that covered the false breast of the imitation Turk.

Dicky wanted to write –'From an unknown friend', but we did not think that was fair, considering how Dicky felt.

So at last we put –'From one who does not wish to sign his name'.

And that was true, at any rate.

Dicky and Oswald lugged the hamper down to the shop that has Carter Paterson's board outside.

'I vote we don't pay the carriage,' said Dicky, but that was perhaps because he was still so very angry about being pulled off the train. Oswald had not had it done to him, so he said that we ought to pay the carriage. And he was jolly glad afterwards that this honourable feeling had arisen in his young bosom, and that he had jolly well made Dicky let it rise in his.

We paid the carriage. It was one-and-five-pence, but Dicky said it was cheap for a high-class revenge like this, and after all it was his money the carriage was paid with.

So then we went home and had another go in of grub – because tea had been rather upset by Dicky's revenge.

The people where we left the hamper told us that it would be delivered next day. So next morning we gloated over the thought of the sell that porter was in for, and Dicky was more deeply gloating than any one.

'I expect it's got there by now,' he said at dinner-time; 'it's a first class booby-trap; what a sell for him! He'll read the list and then he'll take out one parcel after another till he comes to the cake. It *was* a ripping idea! I'm glad I thought of it!'

'I'm not,' said Noël suddenly. 'I wish you hadn't – I wish we hadn't. I know just exactly what he feels like now. He feels as if he'd like to *kill* you for it, and I daresay he would if you hadn't been a craven, white-feathered skulker and not signed your name.'

It was a thunderbolt in our midst Noël behaving like this. It made Oswald feel a sick inside feeling that perhaps Dora had been right. She sometimes is – and Oswald hates this feeling.

Dicky was so surprised at the unheard-of cheek of his young brother that for a moment he was speechless, and before he got over his speechlessness Noël was crying and wouldn't have any more dinner. Alice spoke in the eloquent language of the human eye and begged Dicky to look over it this once. And he replied by means of the same useful organ that he didn't care what a silly kid thought. So no more was said. When Noël had done crying he began to write a piece of poetry and kept at it all the afternoon. Oswald only saw just the beginning. It was called

THE DISAPPOINTED PORTER'S FURY
Supposed to be by the Porter himself,

and it began:

> When first I opened the hamper fair
> And saw the parcel inside there
> My heart rejoiced like dry gardens when
> It rains – but soon I changed and then
> I seized my trusty knife and bowl
> Of poison, and said 'Upon the whole

I will have the life of the man
Or woman who thought of this wicked plan
To deceive a trusting porter so.
No noble heart would have thought of it. No.'

There were pages and pages of it. Of course it was all nonsense – the poetry, I mean. And yet . . . (I have seen that put in books when the author does not want to let out all he thought at the time.)

That evening at tea-time Jane came and said –

'Master Dicky, there's an old aged man at the door inquiring if you live here.'

So Dicky thought it was the bootmaker perhaps; so he went out, and Oswald went with him, because he wanted to ask for a bit of cobbler's wax.

But it was not the shoemaker. It was an old man, pale in the face and white in the hair, and he was so old that we asked him into Father's study by the fire, as soon as we had found out it was really Dicky he wanted to see.

When we got him there he said –

'Might I trouble you to shut the door?'

This is the way a burglar or a murderer might behave, but we did not think he was one. He looked too old for these professions.

When the door was shut, he said –

'I ain't got much to say, young gemmen. It's only to ask was it you sent this?'

He pulled a piece of paper out of his pocket, and it was our list. Oswald and Dicky looked at each other.

'Did you send it?' said the old man again.

So then Dicky shrugged his shoulders and said, 'Yes.'

Oswald said, 'How did you know and who are you?'

The old man got whiter than ever. He pulled out a piece of paper – it was the greenish-grey piece we'd wrapped the Turk and chains in. And it had a label on it that we hadn't

116

noticed, with Dicky's name and address on it. The new bat he got at Christmas had come in it.

'That's how I know,' said the old man. 'Ah, be sure your sin will find you out.'

'But who are you, anyway!' asked Oswald again.

'Oh, *I* ain't nobody in particular,' he said. 'I'm only the father of the pore gell as you took in with your cruel, deceitful, lying tricks. Oh, you may look uppish, young sir, but I'm here to speak my mind, and I'll speak it if I die for it. So now!'

'But we didn't send it to a girl,' said Dicky. 'We wouldn't do such a thing. We sent it for a – for a —' I think he tried to say for a joke, but he couldn't with the fiery way the old man looked at him – 'for a sell, to pay a porter out for stopping me getting into a train when it was just starting, and I missed going to the Circus with the others.' Oswald was glad Dicky was not too proud to explain to the old man. He was rather afraid he might be.

'I never sent it to a girl,' he said again.

'Ho,' said the aged one. 'An' who told you that there porter was a single man? It was his wife – my pore gell – as opened your low parcel, and she sees your lying list written out so plain on top, and, sez she to me, "Father," says she, "'ere's a friend in need! All these good things for us, and no name signed, so that we can't even say thank you. I suppose it's some one knows how short we are just now, and hardly enough to eat with coals the price they are," says she to me. "I do call that kind and Christian," says she, "and I won't open not one of them lovely parcels till Jim comes 'ome," she says, "and we'll enjoy the pleasures of it together, all three of us," says she. And when he came home – we opened of them lovely parcels. She's a cryin' her eyes out at home now, and Jim, he only swore once, and I don't blame him for that one – though never an evil speaker myself – and then he set himself down on a chair and puts his elbows on it to hide his face like – and "Emmie," says he, "so help me. I didn't know I'd got an enemy in the world. I always thought we'd got nothing but good friends," says he. An' I says nothing, but I picks up the paper, and comes here to your fine house to tell you what I think of you. It's a mean, low-down, dirty, nasty trick, and no gentleman wouldn't a-done it. So that's all – and it's off my chest, and good-night to you gentlemen both!'

He turned to go out. I shall not tell you what Oswald felt, except that he did hope Dicky felt the same, and would behave accordingly. And Dicky did, and Oswald was both pleased and surprised.

Dicky said –

'Oh, I say, stop a minute. I didn't think of your poor girl.'

'And her youngest but a bare three weeks old,' said the old man angrily.

'I didn't, on my honour I didn't think of anything but paying the porter out.'

'He was only a doing of his duty,' the old man said.

'Well, I beg your pardon and his,' said Dicky; 'it was ungentlemanly, and I'm very sorry. And I'll try to make it up somehow. Please make it up. I can't do more than own I'm sorry. I wish I hadn't – there!'

'Well,' said the old man slowly, 'we'll leave it at that. Next time p'r'aps you'll think a bit who it's going to be as'll get the benefit of your payings out.'

Dicky made him shake hands, and Oswald did the same.

Then we had to go back to the others and tell them. It was hard. But it was ginger-ale and seed-cake compared to having to tell Father, which was what it came to in the end. For we all saw, though Noël happened to be the one to say it first, that the only way we could really make it up to James Johnson and his poor girl and his poor girl's father, and the baby that was only three weeks old, was to send them a hamper with all the things in it – *real* things, that we had put on the list in the revengeful hamper. And as we had only six-and-sevenpence among us we had to tell Father. Besides, you feel better inside when you have. He talked to us about it a bit, but he is a good father and does not jaw unduly. He advanced our pocket-money to buy a real large Turk-and-chains. And he gave us six bottles of port wine, because he thought that would be better for the poor girl who had the baby than rum or sherry or even sparkling champagne.

We were afraid to send the hamper by Carter Pat. for fear they should think it was another Avenging Take-in. And that was one reason why we took it ourselves in a cab. The other reason was that we wanted to see them open the hamper, and another was that we wanted – at least Dicky wanted – to have it out man to man with the porter and his wife, and tell them himself how sorry he was.

So we got our gardener to find out secretly when that porter was off duty, and when we knew the times we went to his house at one of them.

Then Dicky got out of the cab and went in and said what he had to say. And then we took in the hamper.

And the old man and his daughter and the porter were most awfully decent to us, and the porter's wife said, 'Lor! let bygones be bygones is what *I* say! Why, we wouldn't never have had this handsome present but for the other. Say no more about it, sir, and thank you kindly, I'm sure.'

And we have been friends with them ever since.

We were short of pocket-money for some time, but Oswald does not complain, though the Turk was Dicky's idea entirely. Yet Oswald is just, and he owns that he helped as much as he could in packing the Hamper of the Avenger. Dora paid her share, too, though she wasn't in it. The author does not shrink from owning that this was very decent of Dora.

This is all the story of –

THE TURK IN CHAINS; or,
RICHARD'S REVENGE.

(His name is really Richard, the same as Father's. We only call him Dicky for short.)

THE GOLDEN GONDOLA

ALBERT'S uncle is tremendously clever, and he writes books. I have told how he fled to Southern shores with a lady who is rather nice. His having to marry her was partly our fault, but we did not mean to do it, and we were very sorry for what we had done. But afterwards we thought perhaps it was all for the best, because if left alone he might have married widows, or old German governesses, or Murdstone aunts, like Daisy and Denny have, instead of the fortunate lady that we were the cause of his being married by.

The wedding was just before Christmas, and we were all there. And then they went to Rome for a period of time that is spoken of in books as the honeymoon. You know that H.O., my youngest brother, tried to go too, disguised as the contents of a dress-basket – but was betrayed and brought back.

Conversation often takes place about the things you like, and we often spoke of Albert's uncle.

One day we had a ripping game of hide-and-seek-all-over-the-house-and-all-the-lights-out, sometimes called devil-in-the-dark, and never to be played except when your father and uncle are out, because of the screams which the strongest cannot suppress when caught by 'he' in unexpectedness and total darkness. The girls do not like this game so much as we do. But it is only fair for them to play it. We have more than once played doll's tea-parties to please them.

Well, when the game was over we were panting like dogs

on the hearthrug in front of the common-room fire, and H.O. said –

'I wish Albert's uncle had been here; he does enjoy it so.'

Oswald has sometimes thought Albert's uncle only play-ed to please us. But H.O. may be right.

'I wonder if they often play it in Rome,' H.O. went on. 'That post-card he sent us with the Colly-whats-its-name-on – you know, the round place with the arches. They could have ripping games there –'

'It's not much fun with only two,' said Dicky.

'Besides,' Dora said, 'when people are first married they always sit in balconies and look at the moon, or else at each other's eyes.'

'They ought to know what their eyes look like by this time,' said Dicky.

'I believe they sit and write poetry about their eyes all day, and only look at each other when they can't think of the rhymes,' said Noël.

'I don't believe she knows how, but I'm certain they read aloud to each other out of the poetry books we gave them for wedding presents,' Alice said.

'It would be beastly ungrateful if they didn't, especi-ally with their backs all covered with gold like they are,' said H.O.

'About those books,' said Oswald slowly, now for the first time joining in what was being said; 'of course it was jolly decent of Father to get such ripping presents for us to give them. But I've sometimes wished we'd given Albert's uncle a really truly present that we'd chosen ourselves and bought with our own chink.'

'I wish we could have *done* something for him,' Noël said; 'I'd have killed a dragon for him as soon as look at it, and Mrs Albert's uncle could have been the Princess, and I would have let him have her.'

'Yes,' said Dicky; 'and we just gave rotten books. But it's no use grizzling over it now. It's all over, and he won't get married again while she's alive.'

This was true, for we live in England which is a morganatic empire where more than one wife at a time is not allowed. In the glorious East he might have married again and again and we could have made it all right about the wedding present.

'I wish he was a Turk for some things,' said Oswald, and explained why.

'I don't think *she* would like it,' said Dora.

Oswald explained that if he was a Turk, she would be a Turquoise (I think that is the feminine Turk), and so would be used to lots of wives and be lonely without them.

And just then . . . You know what they say about talking of angels, and hearing their wings? (There is another way of saying this, but it is not polite, as the present author knows.)

Well, just then the postman came, and of course we rushed out, and among Father's dull letters we found one addressed to 'The Bastables Junior'. It had an Italian stamp – not at all a rare one, and it was a poor specimen too, and the post-mark was *Roma*.

That is what the Italians have got into the habit of calling Rome. I have been told that they put the 'a' instead of the 'e' because they like to open their mouths as much as possible in that sunny and agreeable climate.

The letter was jolly – it was just like hearing him talk (I mean reading, not hearing, of course, but reading him talk is not grammar, and if you can't be both sensible and grammarical, it is better to be senseless).

'Well, kiddies,' it began, and it went on to tell us about things he had seen, not dull pictures and beastly old buildings, but amusing incidents of comic nature. The

Italians must be extreme Jugginses for the kind of things he described to be of such everyday occurring. Indeed, Oswald could hardly believe about the soda-water label that the Italian translated for the English traveller so that it said, 'To distrust of the Mineral Waters too fountain-like foaming. They spread the shape.'

Near the end of this letter came this:

You remember the chapter of 'The Golden Gondola' that I wrote for the *People's Pageant* just before I had the honour to lead to the altar, &c. I mean the one that ends in the subterranean passage, with Geraldine's hair down, and her last hope gone, and the three villains stealing upon her with Venetian subtlety in their hearts and Toledo daggers (specially imported) in their garters? I didn't care much for it myself, you remember. I think I must have been thinking of other things when I wrote it. But you, I recollect, consoled me by refusing to regard it as other than 'ripping'. 'Clinking' was, as I recall it, Oswald's consolatory epithet. You'll weep with me, I feel confident, when you hear that my Editor does not share your sentiments. He writes me that it is not up to my usual form. He fears that the public, &c., and he trusts that in the next chapter, &c. Let us hope that the public will, in this matter, take your views, and not his. Oh! for a really discerning public, just like you – you amiable critics! Albert's new aunt is leaning over my shoulder. I can't break her of the distracting habit. How on earth am I ever to write another line? Greetings to all from

ALBERT'S UNCLE AND AUNT.

PS. – She insists on having her name put to this, but of course she didn't write it. I am trying to teach her to spell.
PSS. – Italian spelling, of course.

'And now,' cried Oswald, 'I see it all.'
The others didn't. They often don't when Oswald does.
'Why, don't you see!' he patiently explained, for he

knows that it is vain to be angry with people because they are not so clever as – as other people. 'It's the direct aspiration of Fate. He wants it, does he? Well, he shall have it!'

'What?' said everybody.

'We'll be it.'

'*What?*' was the not very polite remark now repeated by all.

'Why, his discerning public.'

And still they all remained quite blind to what was so clear to Oswald, the astute and discernful.

'It will be much more useful than killing dragons,' Oswald went on, 'especially as there aren't any; and it will be a really truly wedding present – just what we were wishing we'd given him.'

The five others now fell on Oswald and rolled him under the table and sat on his head so that he had to speak loudly and plainly.

'All right! I'll tell you – in words of one syllable if you like. Let go, I say!' And when he had rolled out with the others and the tablecloth that caught on H.O.'s boots and the books and Dora's workbox, and the glass of paint-water that came down with it, he said –

'We will *be* the public. We will all write to the editor of the *People's Pageant* and tell him what we think about the Geraldine chapter. Do mop up that water, Dora; it's running all under where I'm sitting.'

'Don't you think,' said Dora, devoting her handkerchief and Alice's in the obedient way she does not always use, 'that six letters, all signed "Bastable", and all coming from the same house, would be rather – rather –'

'A bit too thick? Yes,' said Alice; 'but of course we'd have all different names and addresses.'

'We might as well do it thoroughly,' said Dicky, 'and send three or four different letters each.'

'And have them posted in different parts of London. Right oh!' remarked Oswald.

'*I* shall write a piece of poetry for mine,' said Noël.

'They ought all to be on different kinds of paper,' said Oswald. 'Let's go out and get the paper directly after tea.'

We did, but we could only get fifteen different kinds of paper and envelopes, though we went to every shop in the village.

At the first shop, when we said, 'Please we want a penn'orth of paper and envelopes of each of all the different kinds you keep,' the lady of the shop looked at us thinly over blue-rimmed spectacles and said, 'What for?'

And H.O. said, 'To write unonymous letters.'

'Anonymous letters are very wrong,' the lady said, and she wouldn't sell us any paper at all.

But at the other places we did not say what it was for, and they sold it us. There were bluey and yellowy and grey and white kinds, and some was violetish with violets on it, and some pink, with roses. The girls took the florivorous ones, which Oswald thinks are unmanly for any but girls, but you excuse their using it. It seems natural to them to mess about like that.

We wrote the fifteen letters, disguising our handwritings as much as we could. It was not easy. Oswald tried to write one of them with his left hand, but the consequences were almost totally unreadable. Besides, if any one could have read it, they would only have thought it was written in an asylum for the insane, the writing was so delirious. So he chucked it.

Noël was only allowed to write one poem. It began –

> *Oh, Geraldine! Oh, Geraldine!*
> *You are the loveliest heroine!*
> *I never read about one before*
> *That made me want to write more*
> *Poetry. And your Venetian eyes,*

They must have been an awful size;
And black and blue, and like your hair,
And your nose and chin were a perfect pair.

and so on for ages.

The other letters were all saying what a beautiful chapter 'Beneath the Doge's Home' was, and how we liked it better than the other chapters before, and how we hoped the next would be like it. We found out when all too late that H.O. had called it the 'Dog's Home'. But we hoped this would pass unnoticed among all the others. We read the reviews of books in the old *Spectators* and *Athenaeums*, and put in the words they say there about other people's books. We said we thought that chapter about Geraldine and the garters was 'subtle' and 'masterly' and 'inevitable' – that it had an 'old-world charm', and was 'redolent of the soil'. We said, too, that we had 'read it with breathless interest from cover to cover', and that it had 'poignant pathos and a convincing realism', and the 'fine flower of delicate sentiment', besides much other rot that the author can't remember.

When all the letters were done we addressed them and stamped them and licked them down, and then we got different people to post them. Our under-gardener, who lives in Greenwich, and the other under-gardener, who lives in Lewisham, and the servants on their evenings out, which they spent in distant spots like Plaistow and Grove Park – each had a letter to post. The piano-tuner was a great catch – he lived in Highgate; and the electric-bell man was Lambeth. So we got rid of all the letters, and watched the post for a reply. We watched for a week, but no answer came.

You think, perhaps, that we were duffers to watch for a reply when we had signed all the letters with fancy names like Daisy Dolman, Everard St Maur, and Sir Cholmondely Marjoribanks, and put fancy addresses on them, like Chatsworth House, Loampit Vale, and The Bungalow,

Eaton Square. But we were not such idiots as you think, dear reader, and you are not so extra clever as you think, either. We had written *one* letter (it had the grandest *Spectator* words in it) on our own letter-paper, with the address on the top and the uncle's coat-of-arms outside the envelope. Oswald's real own name was signed to this letter, and this was the one we looked for the answer to. See?

But that answer did not come. And when three long days had passed away we all felt most awfully stale about it. Knowing the great good we had done for Albert's uncle made our interior feelings very little better, if at all.

And on the fourth day Oswald spoke up and said what was in everybody's inside heart. He said –

'This is futile rot. I vote we write and ask that editor why he doesn't answer letters.'

'He wouldn't answer that one any more than he did the other,' said Noël. 'Why should he? He knows you can't do anything to him for not.'

'Why shouldn't we go and ask him?' H.O. said. 'He couldn't not answer us if we was all there, staring him in the face.'

'I don't suppose he'd see you,' said Dora; 'and it's "were", not "was".'

'The other editor did when I got the guinea for my beautiful poems,' Noël reminded us.

'Yes,' said the thoughtful Oswald; 'but then it doesn't matter how young you are when you're just a poetry-seller. But we're the discerning public now, and he'd think we ought to be grown up. I say, Dora, suppose you rigged yourself up in old Blakie's things. You'd look quite twenty or thirty.'

Dora looked frightened, and said she thought we'd better not.

But Alice said, 'Well, I will, then. I don't care. I'm as tall as Dora. But I won't go alone. Oswald, you'll have to dress up old and come too. Its not much to do for Albert's uncle's sake.'

'You know you'll enjoy it,' said Dora, and she may have wished that she did not so often think that we had better not. However, the dye was now cast, and the remainder of this adventure was doomed to be coloured by the dye we now prepared. (This is an allegory. It means we had burned our boats. And that is another.)

We decided to do the deed next day, and during the evening Dicky and Oswald went out and bought a grey beard and moustache, which was the only thing we could think of to disguise the manly and youthful form of the bold Oswald into the mature shape of a grown-up and discerning public character.

Meanwhile, the girls made tiptoe and brigand-like excursions into Miss Blake's room (she is the housekeeper) and got several things. Among others, a sort of undecided thing like part of a wig, which Miss Blake wears on Sundays. Jane, our housemaid, says it is called a 'transformation', and that duchesses wear them.

We had to be very secret about the dressing-up that night, and to put Blakie's things all back when they had been tried on.

Dora did Alice's hair. She twisted up what little hair Alice has got by natural means, and tied on a long tail of hair that was Miss Blake's too. Then she twisted that up, bun-like, with many hairpins. Then the wiglet, or transformation, was plastered over the front part, and Miss Blake's Sunday hat, which is of a very brisk character, with half a blue bird in it, was placed on top of everything. There were several petticoats used, and a brown dress and some stockings and hankies to stuff it out where it was too big. A black jacket and crimson tie completed the picture. We thought Alice would do.

Then Oswald went out of the room and secretly assumed

his dark disguise. But when he came in with the beard on, and a hat of Father's, the others were not struck with admiration and respect, like he meant them to be. They rolled about, roaring with laughter, and when he crept into Miss Blake's room and turned up the gas a bit, and looked in her long glass, he owned that they were right and that it was no go. He is tall for his age, but that beard made him look like some horrible dwarf; and his hair being so short added to everything. Any idiot could have seen that the beard had not originally flourished where it now was, but had been transplanted from some other place of growth.

And when he laughed, which now became necessary, he really did look most awful. He has read of beards wagging, but he never saw it before.

While he was looking at himself the girls had thought of a new idea.

But Oswald had an inside presentiment that made it some time before he could even consent to listen to it. But at last, when the others reminded him that it was a noble act, and for the good of Albert's uncle, he let them explain the horrid scheme in all its lurid parts.

It was this: That Oswald should consent to be disguised in women's raiments and go with Alice to see the Editor.

No man ever wants to be a woman, and it was a bitter thing for Oswald's pride, but at last he consented. He is glad he is not a girl. You have no idea what it is like to wear petticoats, especially long ones. I wonder that ladies continue to endure their miserable existences. The top parts of the clothes, too, seemed to be too tight and too loose in the wrong places. Oswald's head, also, was terribly in the way. He had no wandering hairs to fasten transformations on to, even if Miss Blake had had another one, which was not the case. But the girls remembered a governess they had once witnessed whose hair was brief as any boy's, so they put a large hat, with a very tight elastic behind, on to Oswald's head, just as it was, and then with a tickly, pussyish, featherish thing round his neck, hanging wobblily down in long ends, he looked more young-lady-like than he will ever feel.

Some courage was needed for the start next day. Things look so different in the daylight.

'Remember Lord Nithsdale coming out of the Tower,' said Alice. 'Think of the great cause and be brave,' and she tied his neck up.

'I'm brave all right,' said Oswald, 'only I do feel such an ass.'

'I feel rather an ape myself,' Alice owned, 'but I've got three-penn'orth of peppermints to inspire us with bravery. It is called Dutch courage, I believe.'

Owing to our telling Jane we managed to get out unseen by Blakie.

All the others would come, too, in their natural appearance, except that we made them wash their hands and faces. We happened to be flush of chink, so we let them come.

'But if you do,' Oswald said, 'you must surround us in a hollow square of four.'

So they did. And we got down to the station all right. But in the train there were two ladies who stared, and porters and people like that came round the window far more than there could be any need for. Oswald's boots must have shown as he got in. He had forgotten to borrow a pair of Jane's, as he had meant to, and the ones he had on were his largest. His ears got hotter and hotter, and it got more and more difficult to manage his feet and hands. He failed to suck any courage, of any nation, from the peppermints.

Owing to the state Oswald's ears were now in, we agreed to take a cab at Cannon Street. We all crammed in some-how, but Oswald saw the driver wink as he put his boot on the step, and the porter who was opening the cab door winked back, and I am sorry to say Oswald forgot that he was a high-born lady, and he told the porter that he had better jolly well stow his cheek. Then several bystanders began to try and be funny, and Oswald knew exactly what particular sort of fool he was being.

But he bravely silenced the fierce warnings of his ears, and when we got to the Editor's address we sent Dick up with a large card that we had written on,

MISS DAISY DOLMAN
and
THE RIGHT HONOURABLE MISS
ETHELTRUDA BUSTLER.
On urgent business.

and Oswald kept himself and Alice concealed in the cab till the return of the messenger.

'All right; you're to go up,' Dicky came back and said; 'but the boy grinned who told me so. You'd better be jolly careful.'

We bolted like rabbits across the pavement and up the Editor's stairs.

He was very polite. He asked us to sit down, and Oswald did. But first he tumbled over the front of his dress because it would get under his boots, and he was afraid to hold it up, not having practised doing this.

'I think I have had letters from you?' said the Editor.

Alice, who looked terrible with the transformation leaning right-ear-ward, said yes, and that we had come to say what a fine, bold conception we thought the Doge's chapter was. This was what we had settled to say, but she needn't have burst out with it like that. I suppose she forgot herself. Oswald, in the agitation of his clothes, could say nothing. The elastic of the hat seemed to be very slowly slipping up the back of his head, and he knew that, if it once passed the bump that backs of heads are made with, the hat would spring from his head like an arrow from a bow. And all would be frustrated.

'Yes,' said the Editor; 'that chapter seems to have had a great success – a wonderful success. I had no fewer than sixteen letters about it, all praising it in unmeasured terms.' He looked at Oswald's boots, which Oswald had neglected to cover over with his petticoats. He now did this.

'It *is* a nice story, you know,' said Alice timidly.

'So it seems,' the gentleman went on. 'Fourteen of the sixteen letters bear the Blackheath postmark. The enthusiasm for the chapter would seem to be mainly local.'

Oswald would not look at Alice. He could not trust himself, with her looking like she did. He knew at once that only the piano-tuner and the electric man had been faithful to their trust. The others had all posted their letters in the pillar-box just outside our gate. They wanted to get rid of them as quickly as they could, I suppose. Selfishness is a vile quality.

The author cannot deny that Oswald now wished he hadn't. The elastic was certainly moving, slowly, but too surely. Oswald tried to check its career by swelling out the bump on the back of his head, but he could not think of the right way to do this.

'I am very pleased to see you,' the Editor went on slowly, and there was something about the way he spoke that made Oswald think of a cat playing with a mouse. 'Perhaps you can tell me. Are there many spiritualists in Blackheath? Many clairvoyants?'

'Eh?' said Alice, forgetting that that is not the way to behave.

'People who foretell the future?' he said.

'I don't think so,' said Alice. 'Why?'

His eye twinkled. Oswald saw he had wanted her to ask this.

'Because,' said the Editor, more slowly than ever, 'I think

there must be. How otherwise can we account for that chapter about the "Doge's Home" being read and admired by sixteen different people before it is even printed. That chapter has not been printed, it has not been published; it will not be published till the May number of the *People's Pageant*. Yet in Blackheath sixteen people already appreciate its subtlety and its realism and all the rest of it. How do you account for this, Miss Daisy Dolman?'

'I am the Right Honourable Etheltruda,' said Alice. 'At least – oh, it's no use going on. We are not what we seem.'

'Oddly enough, I inferred that at the very beginning of our interview,' said the Editor.

Then the elastic finished slipping up Oswald's head at the back, and the hat leapt from his head exactly as he had known it would. He fielded it deftly, however, and it did not touch the ground.

'Concealment,' said Oswald, 'is at an end.'

'So it appears,' said the Editor. 'Well, I hope next time the author of the "Golden Gondola" will choose his instruments more carefully.'

'He didn't! We aren't!' cried Alice, and she instantly told the Editor everything.

Concealment being at an end, Oswald was able to get at his trousers pocket – it did not matter now how many boots he showed – and to get out Albert's uncle's letter.

Alice was quite eloquent, especially when the Editor had made her take off the hat with the blue bird, and the transformation and the tail, so that he could see what she really looked like. He was quite decent when he really understood how Albert's uncle's threatened marriage must have upset his brain while he was writing that chapter, and pondering on the dark future.

He began to laugh then, and kept it up till the hour of parting.

He advised Alice not to put on the transformation and the tail again to go home in, and she didn't.

Then he said to me: 'Are you in a finished state under Miss Daisy Dolman?' and when Oswald said, 'Yes,' the Editor helped him to take off all the womanly accoutrements, and to do them up in brown paper. And he lent him a cap to go home in.

I never saw a man laugh more. He is an excellent sort.

But no slow passage of years, however many, can ever weaken Oswald's memory of what those petticoats were like to walk in, and how ripping it was to get out of them, and have your own natural legs again.

We parted from the Editor without a strain on anybody's character.

He must have written to Albert's uncle, and told him all, for we got a letter next week. It said –

MY DEAR KIDDIES, – Art cannot be forced. Nor can Fame. May I beg you for the future to confine your exertions to blowing my trumpet – or Fame's – with your natural voices? Editors may be led, but they won't be druv. The Right Honourable Miss Etheltruda Bustler seems to have aroused a deep pity for me in my Editor's heart. Let that suffice. And for the future permit me, as firmly as affectionately, to reiterate the assurance and the advice which I have so often breathed in your long young ears, '*I am not ungrateful; but I do wish you would mind your own business.*'

'That's just because we were found out,' said Alice. 'If we'd succeeded he'd have been sitting on the top of the pinnacle of Fame, and he would have owed it all to us. That would have been making him something like a wedding present.'

What we had really done was to make something very like – but the author is sure he has said enough.

THE FLYING LODGER

FATHER knows a man called Eustace Sandal. I do not know how to express his inside soul, but I have heard Father say he means well. He is a vegetarian and a Primitive Social Something, and an all-wooler, and things like that, and he is really as good as he can stick, only most awfully dull. I believe he eats bread and milk from choice. Well, he has great magnificent dreams about all the things you can do for other people, and he wants to distil cultivatedness into the sort of people who live in Model Workmen's Dwellings, and teach them to live up to better things. This is what he says. So he gives concerts in Camberwell, and places like that, and curates come from far and near, to sing about Bold Bandaleros and the Song of the Bow, and people who have escaped being curates give comic recitings, and he is sure that it does every one good, and 'gives them glimpses of the Life Beautiful'. He said that. Oswald heard him with his own trustworthy ears. Anyway the people enjoy the concerts no end, and that's the great thing.

Well, he came one night, with a lot of tickets he wanted to sell, and Father bought some for the servants, and Dora happened to go in to get the gum for a kite we were making, and Mr Sandal said, 'Well, my little maiden, would you not like to come on Thursday evening, and share in the task of raising our poor brothers and sisters to the higher levels of culture?' So of course Dora said she would, very much. Then he explained about the concert, calling her 'My little one', and 'dear child', which Alice never would have borne, but Dora is not of a sensitive nature, and hardly minds what she is called, so long as it is not names, which she does not deem 'dear child' and cetera to be, though Oswald would.

Dora was quite excited about it, and the stranger so worked upon her feelings that she accepted the deep responsibility of selling tickets, and for a week there was no bearing her. I believe she did sell nine, to people in Lewisham and New Cross who knew no better. And Father bought tickets for all of us, and when the eventful evening dawned we went to Camberwell by train and tram *via* Miss Blake (that means we shouldn't have been allowed to go without her).

The tram ride was rather jolly, but when we got out and walked we felt like 'Alone in London', or 'Jessica's First Prayer', because Camberwell is a devastating region that makes you think of rickety attics with the wind whistling through them, or miserable cellars where forsaken children do wonders by pawning their relations' clothes and looking after the baby. It was a dampish night, and we walked on greasy mud. And as we walked along Alice kicked against something on the pavement, and it chinked, and when she picked it up it was five bob rolled up in newspaper.

'I expect it's somebody's little all,' said Alice, 'and the cup was dashed from their lips just when they were going to joyfully spend it. We ought to give it to the police.'

But Miss Blake said no, and that we were late already, so we went on, and Alice held the packet in her muff throughout the concert which ensued. I will not tell you anything about the concert except that it was quite fairly jolly – you must have been to these Self-Raising Concerts in the course of your young lives.

When it was over we reasoned with Miss Blake, and she let us go through the light blue paper door beside the stage and find Mr Sandal. We thought he might happen to hear who had lost the five bob, and return it to its sorrowing family. He was in a great hurry, but he took the chink and said he'd let us know if anything happened. Then we went home very cheerful, singing bits of the comic songs a bishop's son had done in the concert, and little thinking what we were taking home with us.

It was only a few days after this, or perhaps a week, that we all began to be rather cross. Alice, usually as near a brick as a girl can go, was the worst of the lot, and if you said what you thought of her she instantly began to snivel. And we all had awful colds, and our handkerchiefs gave out, and then our heads ached. Oswald's head was particularly hot, I remember, and he wanted to rest it on the backs of chairs or on tables – or anything steady.

But why prolong the painful narrative? What we had brought home from Camberwell was the measles, and as soon as the grown-ups recognized the Grim Intruder for the fell disease it is we all went to bed, and there was an end of active adventure for some time.

Of course, when you begin to get better there are grapes and other luxuries not of everyday occurrences, but while you're sniffling and fevering in bed, as red as a lobster and blazing hot, you are inclined to think it is a heavy price to pay for any concert, however raising.

Mr Sandal came to see Father the very day we all marched Bedward. He had found the owner of the five shillings. It was a doctor's fee, about to be paid by the parent of a thoroughly measly family. And if we had taken it to the police at once Alice would not have held it in her hand all through the concert – but I will not blame Blakie. She was a jolly good nurse, and read aloud to us with unfatigu-able industry while we were getting better.

Our having fallen victims to this disgusting complaint ended in our being sent to the seaside. Father could not take us himself, so we went to stay with a sister of Mr Sandal's. She was like him, only more so in every way.

The journey was very joyous. Father saw us off at

Cannon Street, and we had a carriage to ourselves all the way, and we passed the station where Oswald would not like to be a porter. Rude boys at this station put their heads out of the window and shout, 'Who's a duffer?' and things like that, and the porters have to shout 'I am!' because Higham is the name of the station, and porters seldom have any H's with which to protect themselves from this cruel joke.

It was a glorious moment when the train swooped out of a tunnel and we looked over the downs and saw the grey-blue line that was the sea. We had not seen the sea since before Mother died. I believe we older ones all thought of that, and it made us quieter than the younger ones were. I do not want to forget anything, but it makes you feel empty and stupid when you remember some things.

There was a good drive in a waggonette after we got to our station. There were primroses under some of the hedges, and lots of dog-violets. And at last we got to Miss Sandal's house. It is before you come to the village, and it is a little square white house. There is a big old windmill at the back of it. It is not used any more for grinding corn, but fishermen keep their nets in it.

Miss Sandal came out of the green gate to meet us. She had a soft, drab dress and a long thin neck, and her hair was drab too, and it was screwed up tight.

She said, 'Welcome, one and all!' in a kind voice, but it was too much like Mr Sandal's for me. And we went in. She showed us the sitting-rooms, and the rooms where we were to sleep, and then she left us to wash our hands and faces. When we were alone we burst open the doors of our rooms with one consent, and met on the landing with a rush like the great rivers of America.

'*Well!*' said Oswald, and the others said the same.

'Of all the rummy cribs!' remarked Dicky.

'It's like a workhouse or a hospital,' said Dora. 'I think I like it.'

'It makes me think of bald-headed gentlemen,' said H.O., 'it is so bare.'

It was. All the walls were white plaster, the furniture was white deal – what there was of it, which was precious little. There were no carpets – only white matting. And there was not a single ornament in a single room! There was a clock on the dining-room mantelpiece, but that could not be counted as an ornament because of the useful side of its character. There were only about six pictures – all of a brownish colour. One was the blind girl sitting on an orange with a broken fiddle. It is called Hope.

When we were clean Miss Sandal gave us tea. As we sat down she said, 'The motto of our little household is "Plain living and high thinking".'

And some of us feared for an instant that this might mean not enough to eat. But fortunately this was not the case. There was plenty, but all of a milky, bunny, fruity, vegetable sort. We soon got used to it, and liked it all right.

Miss Sandal was very kind. She offered to read aloud to us after tea, and, exchanging glances of despair, some of us said that we should like it very much.

It was Oswald who found the manly courage to say very politely –

'Would it be all the same to you if we went and looked at the sea first? Because –'

And she said, 'Not at all,' adding something about 'Nature, the dear old nurse, taking somebody on her knee,' and let us go.

We asked her which way, and we tore up the road and through the village and on to the sea-wall, and then with six joyous bounds we leaped down on to the sand.

The author will not bother you with a description of the mighty billows of ocean, which you must have read about, if not seen, but he will just say what perhaps you are not aware of – that seagulls eat clams and mussels and cockles, and crack the shells with their beaks. The author has seen this done.

You also know, I suppose, that you can dig in the sand (if you have a spade) and make sand castles, and stay in them till the tide washes you out.

I will say no more, except that when we gazed upon the sea and the sand we felt we did not care tuppence how highly Miss Sandal might think of us or how plainly she might make us live, so long as we had got the briny deep to go down to.

It was too early in the year and too late in the day to bathe, but we paddled, which comes to much the same thing, and you almost always have to change everything afterwards.

When it got dark we had to go back to the White House, and there was supper, and then we found that Miss Sandal did not keep a servant, so of course we offered to help wash up. H.O. only broke two plates.

Nothing worth telling about happened till we had been over there a week, and had got to know the coastguards and a lot of the village people quite well. I do like coastguards. They seem to know everything you want to hear about. Miss Sandal used to read to us out of poetry books, and about a chap called Thoreau, who could tickle fish, and they liked it, and let him. She was kind, but rather like her house – there was something bare and bald about her inside mind, I believe. She was very, very calm, and said that people who lost their tempers were not living the higher life. But one day a telegram came, and then she was not calm at all. She got quite like other people, and quite shoved H.O. for getting in her way when she was looking for her purse to pay for the answer to the telegram.

Then she said to Dora – and she was pale and her eyes

red, just like people who live the lower or ordinary life – 'My dears, it's dreadful! My poor brother! He's had a fall. I must go to him *at once*.' And she sent Oswald to order the fly from the Old Ship Hotel, and the girls to see if Mrs Beale would come and take care of us while she was away. Then she kissed us all and went off very unhappy. We heard afterwards that poor, worthy Mr Sandal had climbed a scaffolding to give a workman a tract about drink, and he didn't know the proper part of the scaffolding to stand on (the workman did, of course) so he fetched down half a dozen planks and the workman, and if a dust-cart hadn't happened to be passing just under so that they fell into it their lives would not have been spared. As it was Mr Sandal broke his arm and his head. The workman escaped unscathed but furious. The workman was a tee-totaler.

Mrs Beale came, and the first thing she did was to buy a leg of mutton and cook it. It was the first meat we had had since arriving at Lymchurch.

'I 'spect she can't afford good butcher's meat,' said Mrs Beale; 'but your pa, I expect he pays for you, and I lay he'd like you to have your fill of something as'll lay acrost your chesties.' So she made a Yorkshire pudding as well. It was good.

After dinner we sat on the sea-wall, feeling more like after dinner than we had felt for days, and Dora said –

'Poor Miss Sandal! I never thought about her being hard-up, somehow. I wish we could do something to help her.'

'We might go out street-singing,' Noël said. But that was no good, because there is only one street in the village, and the people there are much too poor for one to be able to ask them for anything. And all round it is fields with only sheep, who have nothing to give except their wool, and when it comes to taking that, they are never asked.

Dora thought we might get Father to give her money, but Oswald knew this would never do.

Then suddenly a thought struck some one – I will not say who – and that some one said –

'She ought to let lodgings, like all the other people do in Lymchurch.'

That was the beginning of it. The end – for that day – was our getting the top of a cardboard box and printing on it the following lines in as many different coloured chalks as we happened to have with us.

LODGINGS TO LET.

INQUIRE INSIDE.

We ruled spaces for the letters to go in, and did it very neatly. When we went to bed we stuck it in our bedroom window with stamp-paper.

In the morning when Oswald drew up his blind there was quite a crowd of kids looking at the card. Mrs Beale came out and shoo-ed them away as if they were hens. And we did not have to explain the card to her at all. She never said anything about it. I never knew such a woman as Mrs Beale for minding her own business. She said afterwards she supposed Miss Sandal had told us to put up the card.

Well, two or three days went by, and nothing happened, only we had a letter from Miss Sandal, telling us how the poor sufferer was groaning, and one from Father telling us to be good children, and not get into scrapes. And people who drove by used to look at the card and laugh.

And then one day a carriage came driving up with a gentleman in it, and he saw the rainbow beauty of our chalked card, and he got out and came up the path. He had a pale face, and white hair and very bright eyes that moved about quickly like a bird's, and he was dressed in a quite new tweed suit that did not fit him very well.

Dora and Alice answered the door before any one had time to knock, and the author has reason to believe their hearts were beating wildly.

'How much?' said the gentleman shortly.

Alice and Dora were so surprised by his suddenness that they could only reply –

'Er – er –'

'Just so,' said the gentleman briskly as Oswald stepped modestly forward and said –

'Won't you come inside?'

'The very thing,' said he, and came in.

We showed him into the dining-room and asked him to excuse us a minute, and then held a breathless council outside the door.

'It depends how many rooms he wants,' said Dora.

'Let's say so much a room,' said Dicky, 'and extra if he wants Mrs Beale to wait on him.'

So we decided to do this. We thought a pound a room seemed fair.

And we went back.

'How many rooms do you want?' Oswald asked.

'All the room there is,' said the gentleman.

'They are a pound each,' said Oswald, 'and extra for Mrs Beale.'

'How much altogether?'

Oswald thought a minute and then said 'Nine rooms is nine pounds, and two pounds a week for Mrs Beale, because she is a widow.'

'Done!' said the gentleman. 'I'll go and fetch my port-manteaus.'

He bounced up and out and got into his carriage and drove away. It was not till he was finally gone quite beyond recall that Alice suddenly said –

'But if he has all the rooms where are *we* to sleep?'

'He must be awfully rich,' said H.O., 'wanting all those rooms.'

'Well, he can't sleep in more than one at once,' said Dicky, 'however rich he is. We might wait till he was bedded down and then sleep in the rooms he didn't want.'

But Oswald was firm. He knew that if the man paid for the rooms he must have them to himself.

'He won't sleep in the kitchen,' said Dora; 'couldn't we sleep there?'

But we all said we couldn't and wouldn't.

Then Alice suddenly said –

'I know! The Mill. There are heaps and heaps of fishing-nets there, and we could each take a blanket like Indians and creep over under cover of the night after the Beale has gone, and get back before she comes in the morning.'

It seemed a sporting thing to do, and we agreed. Only Dora said she thought it would be draughty.

Of course we went over to the Mill at once to lay our plans and prepare for the silent watches of the night.

There are three stories to a windmill, besides the ground-floor. The first floor is pretty empty; the next is nearly full of millstones and machinery, and the one above is where the corn runs down from on to the millstones.

We settled to let the girls have the first floor, which was covered with heaps of nets, and we would pig in with the millstones on the floor above.

We had just secretly got out the last of the six blankets from the house and got it into the Mill disguised in a clothes-basket, when we heard wheels, and there was the gentleman back again. He had only got one portmanteau after all, and that was a very little one.

Mrs Beale was bobbing at him in the doorway when we got up. Of course we had told her he had rented rooms, but we had not said how many, for fear she should ask where we were going to sleep, and we had a feeling that but few grown-ups would like our sleeping in a mill, however much we were living the higher life by sacrificing ourselves to get money for Miss Sandal.

The gentleman ordered sheep's-head and trotters for dinner, and when he found he could not have that he said –

'Gammon and spinach!'

But there was not any spinach in the village, so he had to fall back on eggs and bacon. Mrs Beale cooked it, and when he had fallen back on it she washed up and went home. And we were left. We could hear the gentleman singing to himself, something about woulding he was a bird that he might fly to thee.

Then we got the lanterns that you take when you go 'up street' on a dark night, and we crept over to the Mill. It was much darker than we expected.

We decided to keep our clothes on, partly for warmness and partly in case of any sudden alarm or the fishermen wanting their nets in the middle of the night, which sometimes happens if the tide is favourable.

We let the girls keep the lantern, and we went up with a bit of candle Dicky had saved, and tried to get comfortable among the millstones and machinery, but it was not easy, and Oswald, for one, was not sorry when he heard the voice of Dora calling in trembling tones from the floor below.

'Oswald! Dicky!' said the voice, 'I wish one of you would come down a sec.'

Oswald flew to the assistance of his distressed sister.

'It's only that we're a little bit uncomfortable,' she whispered. 'I didn't want to yell it out because of Noël and H.O. I don't want to frighten them, but I can't help feeling that if anything popped out of the dark at us I should die. Can't you all come down here? The nets are quite comfortable, and I do wish you would.'

Alice said she was not frightened, but suppose there were

rats, which are said to infest old buildings, especially mills?

So we consented to come down, and we told Noël and H.O. to come down because it was more comfy, and it is easier to settle yourself for the night among fishing-nets than among machinery. There *was* a rustling now and then among the heap of broken chairs and jack-planes and baskets and spades and hoes and bits of the spars of ships at the far end of our sleeping apartment, but Dicky and Oswald resolutely said it was the wind or else jackdaws making their nests, though, of course, they knew this is not done at night.

Sleeping in a mill was not nearly the fun we had thought it would be – somehow. For one thing, it was horrid not having a pillow, and the fishing-nets were so stiff you could not bunch them up properly to make one. And unless you have been born and bred a Red Indian you do not know how to manage your blanket so as to make it keep out the draughts. And when we had put out the light Oswald more than once felt as though earwigs and spiders were walking on his face in the dark, but when we struck a match there was nothing there.

And empty mills do creak and rustle and move about in a very odd way. Oswald was not afraid, but he did think we might as well have slept in the kitchen, because the gentleman could not have wanted to use that when he was asleep. You see, we thought then that he would sleep all night like other people.

We got to sleep at last, and in the night the girls edged up to their bold brothers, so that when the morning sun 'shone in bars of dusty gold through the chinks of the aged edifice' and woke us up we were all lying in a snuggly heap like a litter of puppies.

'Oh, I *am* so stiff!' said Alice, stretching. 'I never slept in my clothes before. It makes me feel as if I had been starched and ironed like a boy's collar.'

We all felt pretty much the same. And our faces were tired too, and stiff, which was rum, and the author cannot account for it, unless it really was spiders that walked on us. I believe the ancient Greeks considered them to be venomous, and perhaps that's how their venom influences their victims.

'I think mills are merely beastly,' remarked H.O. when we had woke him up. 'You can't wash yourself or brush your hair or anything.'

'You aren't always so jolly particular about your hair,' said Dicky.

'Don't be so disagreeable,' said Dora.

And Dicky rejoined, 'Disagreeable yourself!'

There is certainly something about sleeping in your clothes that makes you feel not so kind and polite as usual. I expect this is why tramps are so fierce and knock people down in lonely roads and kick them. Oswald knows he felt just like kicking any one if they had happened to cheek him the least little bit. But by a fortunate accident nobody did.

The author believes there is a picture called 'Hopeless Dawn'. We felt exactly like that. Nothing seemed the least bit of good.

It was a pitiful band with hands and faces dirtier than any one would believe who had not slept in a mill or witnessed others who had done so, that crossed the wet, green grass between the Mill and the white house.

'I shan't ever put morning dew into my poetry again,' Noël said; 'it is not nearly so poetical as people make out, and it is as cold as ice, right through your boots.'

We felt rather better when we had had a good splash in the brick-paved back kitchen that Miss Sandal calls the bath-room. And Alice made a fire and boiled a kettle and we had some tea and eggs. Then we looked at the clock and it was half-past five. So we hastened to get into another part of the house before Mrs Beale came.

'I wish we'd tried to live the higher life some less beastly way,' said Dicky as we went along the passage.

'Living the higher life always hurts at the beginning,' Alice said. 'I expect it's like new boots, only when you've got used to it you're glad you bore it at first. Let's listen at the doors till we find out where he isn't sleeping.'

So we listened at all the bedroom doors, but not a snore was heard.

'Perhaps he was a burglar,' said H.O., 'and only pretended to want lodgings so as to get in and bone all the valuables.'

'There aren't any valuables,' said Noël, and this was quite true, for Miss Sandal had no silver or jewellery except a brooch of pewter, and the very teaspoons were of wood – very hard to keep clean and having to be scraped.

'Perhaps he sleeps without snoring,' said Oswald, 'some people do.'

'Not old gentlemen,' said Noël; 'think of our Indian uncle – H.O. used to think it was bears at first.'

'Perhaps he rises with the lark,' said Alice, 'and is wondering why brekker isn't ready.'

So then we listened at the sitting-room doors, and through the keyhole of the parlour we heard a noise of some one moving, and then in a soft whistle the tune of the 'Would I were a bird' song.

So then we went into the dining-room to sit down. But when we opened the door we almost fell in a heap on the matting, and no one had breath for a word – not even for 'Crikey', which was what we all thought.

I have read of people who could not believe their eyes; and I have always thought it such rot of them, but now, as the author gazed on the scene, he really could not be quite sure that he was not in a dream, and that the gentleman and the night in the Mill weren't dreams too.

'Pull back the curtains,' Alice said, and we did. I wish

I could make the reader feel as astonished as we did.

The last time we had seen the room the walls had been bare and white. Now they were covered with the most splendid drawings you can think of, all done in coloured chalk – I don't mean mixed up, like we do with our chalks – but one picture was done in green, and another in brown, and another in red, and so on. And the chalk must have been of some fat radiant kind quite unknown to us, for some of the lines were over an inch thick.

'How perfectly *lovely*!' Alice said; 'he must have sat up all night to do it. He *is* good. I expect he's trying to live the higher life, too – just going about doing secretly, and spending his time making other people's houses pretty.'

'I wonder what he'd have done if the room had had a large pattern of brown roses on it, like Mrs Beale's,' said Noël. 'I say, *look* at that angel! Isn't it poetical? It makes me feel I must write something about it.'

It *was* a good angel – all drawn in grey, that was – with very wide wings going right across the room, and a whole bundle of lilies in his arms. Then there were seagulls and ravens, and butterflies, and ballet girls with butterflies' wings, and a man with artificial wings being fastened on, and you could see he was just going to jump off a rock. And there were fairies, and bats, and flying-foxes, and flying-fish. And one glorious winged horse done in red chalk – and his wings went from one side of the room to the other, and crossed the angel's. There were dozens and dozens of birds – all done in just a few lines – but exactly right. You couldn't make any mistake about what anything was meant for.

And all the things, whatever they were, had wings to them. How Oswald wishes that those pictures had been done in his house!

While we stood gazing, the door of the other room opened, and the gentleman stood before us, more covered with different-coloured chalks than I should have thought he could have got, even with all those drawings, and he had a thing made of wire and paper in his hand, and he said –

'Wouldn't you like to fly?'

'Yes,' said every one.

'Well then,' he said, 'I've got a nice little flying-machine here. I'll fit it on to one of you, and then you jump out of the attic window. You don't know what it's like to fly.'

We said we would rather not.

'But I insist,' said the gentleman. 'I have your real interest at heart, my children – I can't allow you in your ignorance to reject the chance of a lifetime.'

We still said 'No, thank you,' and we began to feel very uncomfy, for the gentleman's eyes were now rolling wildly.

'Then I'll *make* you!' he said, catching hold of Oswald.

'You jolly well won't,' cried Dicky, catching hold of the arm of the gentleman.

Then Dora said very primly and speaking rather slowly, and she was very pale –

'I think it would be lovely to fly. Will you just show me how the flying-machine looks when it is unfolded?'

The gentleman dropped Oswald, and Dora made 'Go! go' with her lips without speaking, while he began to unfold the flying-machine. We others went, Oswald lingering last, and then in an instant Dora had nipped out of the room and banged the door and locked it.

'To the Mill!' she cried, and we ran like mad, and got in and barred the big door, and went up to the first floor, and looked out of the big window to warn off Mrs Beale.

And we thumped Dora on the back, and Dicky called her a Sherlock Holmes, and Noël said she was a heroine.

'It wasn't anything,' Dora said, just before she began to cry, 'only I remember reading that you must pretend to humour them, and then get away, for of course I saw at once he was a lunatic. Oh, how awful it might have been! He could have made us all jump out of the attic window, and there would have been no one left to tell Father. Oh! oh!' and then the crying began.

But we were proud of Dora, and I am sorry we make fun of her sometimes, but it is difficult not to.

We decided to signal the first person that passed, and we got Alice to take off her red flannel petticoat for a signal.

The first people who came were two men in a dog-cart. We waved the signalizing petticoat and they pulled up, and one got out and came up to the Mill.

We explained about the lunatic and the wanting us to jump out of the windows.

'Right oh!' cried the man to the one still in the cart; 'got him.' And the other hitched the horse to the gate and came over, and the other went to the house.

'Come along down, young ladies and gentlemen,' said the second man when he had been told. 'He's as gentle as a lamb. He does not think it hurts to jump out of windows. He thinks it really is flying. He'll be like an angel when he sees the doctor.'

We asked if he had been mad before, because we had thought he might have suddenly gone so.

'Certainly he has!' replied the man; 'he has never been, so to say, himself since tumbling out of a flying-machine he went up in with a friend. He was an artist previous to that – an excellent one, I believe. But now he only draws objects with wings – and now and then he wants to make people fly – perfect strangers sometimes, like yourselves. Yes, miss, I am his attendant, and his pictures often amuse me by the half-hours together, poor gentleman.'

'How did he get away?' Alice asked

'Well, miss, the poor gentleman's brother got hurt and Mr Sidney – that's him inside – seemed wonderfully put out and hung over the body in a way pitiful to see. But really he was extracting the cash from the sufferer's pockets. Then, while all of us were occupied with Mr Eustace, Mr Sidney just packs his portmanteau and out he goes by the back door. When we missed him we sent for Dr Baker, but by the time he came it was too late to get here. Dr Baker said at once he'd revert to his boyhood's home. And the doctor has proved correct.'

We had all come out of the Mill, and with this polite person we went to the gate, and saw the lunatic into the carriage, very gentle and gay.

'But, Doctor,' Oswald said, 'he did say he'd give nine pounds a week for the rooms. Oughtn't he to pay?'

'You might have known he was mad to say that,' said the doctor. 'No. Why should he, when it's his own sister's house? Gee up!'

And he left us.

It was sad to find the gentleman was not a Higher Life after all, but only mad. And I was more sorry than ever for poor Miss Sandal. As Oswald pointed out to the girls they are much more blessed in their brothers than Miss Sandal is, and they ought to be more grateful than they are.

THE SMUGGLER'S REVENGE

THE days went on and Miss Sandal did not return. We went on being very sorry about Miss Sandal being so poor, and it was not our fault that when we tried to let the house in lodgings, the first lodger proved to be a lunatic of the deepest dye. Miss Sandal must have been a fairly decent sort, because she seems not to have written to Father about it. At any rate he didn't give it us in any of our letters, about our good intentions and their ending in a maniac.

Oswald does not like giving up a thing just because it has once been muffed. The muffage of a plan is a thing that often happens at first to heroes – like Bruce and the spider, and other great characters. Besides, grown-ups always say –

'If at first you don't succeed,
Try, try, try again!'

And if this is the rule for Euclid and rule-of-three and all the things you would rather not do, think how much more it must be the rule when what you are after is your own idea, and not just the rotten notion of that beast Euclid, or the unknown but equally unnecessary author who composed the multiplication table. So we often talked about what we could do to make Miss Sandal rich. It gave us something to jaw about when we happened to want to sit down for a bit, in between all the glorious wet sandy games that happen by the sea.

Of course if we wanted real improving conversation we used to go up to the boat-house and talk to the coastguards.

I do think coastguards are A1. They are just the same as sailors, having been so in their youth, and you can get at them to talk to, which is not the case with sailors who are at sea (or even in harbours) on ships. Even if you had the luck to get on to a man-of-war, you would very likely not be able to climb to the top-gallants to talk to the man there. Though in books the young hero always seems able to climb to the mast-head the moment he is told to. The coastguards told us tales of Southern ports, and of shipwrecks, and officers they had *not* cottoned to, and the messmates that they *had*, but when we asked them about smuggling they said there wasn't any to speak of nowadays.

'I expect they think they oughtn't to talk about such dark crimes before innocent kids like us,' said Dicky afterwards, and he grinned as he said it.

'Yes,' said Alice; 'they don't know how much we know about smugglers, and bandits, and highwaymen, and burglars, and coiners,' and she sighed, and we all felt sad to think that we had not now any chance to play at being these things.

'We might play smugglers,' said Oswald.

But he did not speak hopefully. The worst of growing up is that you seem to want more and more to have a bit of the real thing in your games. Oswald could not now be content to play at bandits and just capture Albert next door, as once, in happier days, he was pleased and proud to do.

It was not a coastguard that told us about the smugglers. It was a very old man that we met two or three miles along the beach. He was leaning against a boat that was wrong way up on the shingle, and smoking the strongest tobacco Oswald's young nose has ever met. I think it must have been Black Jack. We said, 'How do you do?' and Alice said, 'Do you mind if we sit down near you?'

'Not me,' replied the aged seafarer. We could see directly that he was this by his jersey and his sea-boots.

The girls sat down on the beach, but we boys leaned against the boat like the seafaring one. We hoped he would join in conversation, but at first he seemed too proud. And there was something dignified about him, bearded and like a Viking, that made it hard for us to begin.

At last he took his pipe out of his mouth and said –

'Here's a precious Quakers' meeting! You didn't set down here just for to look at me?'

'I'm sure you look very nice,' Dora said.

'Same to you, miss, I'm sure,' was the polite reply.

'We want to talk to you awfully,' said Alice, 'if you don't mind?'

'Talk away,' said he.

And then, as so often happens, no one could think of anything to say.

Suddenly Noël said, '*I* think you look nice too, but I think you look as though you had a secret history. Have you?'

'Not me,' replied the Viking-looking stranger. 'I ain't got no history, nor joggraphy neither. They didn't give us that much schooling when I was a lad.'

'Oh!' replied Noël; 'but what I really meant was, were you ever a pirate or anything?'

'Never in all my born,' replied the stranger, now thoroughly roused; 'I'd scorn the haction. I was in the navy, I was, till I lost the sight of my eye, looking too close at gunpowder. Pirates is snakes, and they ought to be killed as such.'

We felt rather sorry, for though of course it is very wrong to be a pirate, it is very interesting too. Things are often like this. That is one of the reasons why it is so hard to be truly good.

Dora was the only one who was pleased. She said –

'Yes, pirates *are* very wrong. And so are highwaymen and smugglers.'

'I don't know about highwaymen,' the old man replied; 'they went out afore my time, worse luck; but my father's great-uncle by the mother's side, he see one hanged once. A fine upstanding fellow he was, and made a speech while they was a-fitting of the rope. All the women were snivelling and sniffing and throwing bokays at him.'

'Did any of the bouquets reach him?' asked the interested Alice.

'Not likely,' said the old man. 'Women can't never shy straight. But I shouldn't wonder but what them posies heartened the chap up a bit. An afterwards they was all a-fightin' to get a bit of the rope he was hung with, for luck.'

'Do tell us some more about him,' said all of us but Dora.

'I don't know no more about him. He was just hung – that's all. They was precious fond o' hangin' in them old far-away times.'

'Did you ever know a smuggler?' asked H.O. – 'to speak to, I mean?'

'Ah, that's tellings,' said the old man, and he winked at us all.

So then we instantly knew that the coastguards had been mistaken when they said there were no more smugglers now, and that this brave old man would not betray his comrades, even to friendly strangers like us. But of course he could not know exactly how friendly we were. So we told him.

Oswald said –

'We *love* smugglers. We wouldn't even tell a word about it if you would only tell us.'

'There used to be lots of smuggling on these here coasts when my father was a boy,' he said; 'my own father's cousin, his father took to the smuggling, and he was a doin' so well at it, that what does he do, but goes and gets married, and the Preventives they goes and nabs him on his wedding-day, and walks him straight off from the church door, and claps him in Dover Jail.'

'Oh, his poor wife,' said Alice, 'whatever did she do?'

'*She* didn't do nothing,' said the old man. 'It's a woman's place not to do nothing till she's told to. He'd done so well at the smuggling, he'd saved enough by his honest toil to take a little public. So she sets there awaitin' and attendin' to customers – for well she knowed him, as he wasn't the chap to let a bit of a jail stand in the way of his station in life. Well, it was three weeks to a day after the wedding, there comes a dusty chap to the "Peal of Bells" door. That was the sign over the public, you understand.'

We said we did, and breathlessly added, 'Go on!'

'A dusty chap he was; got a beard and a patch over one eye, and he come of a afternoon when there was no one about the place but her.

'"Hullo, missis," says he; "got a room for a quiet chap?"

'"I don't take in no men-folks," says she; "can't be bothered with 'em."

'"You'll be bothered with me, if I'm not mistaken," says he.

'"Bothered if I will," says she.

'"Bothered if you won't," says he, and with that he ups with his hand and off comes the black patch, and he pulls off the beard and gives her a kiss and a smack on the shoulder. She always said she nearly died when she see it was her new-made bridegroom under the beard.

'So she took her own man in as a lodger, and he went to work up at Upton's Farm with his beard on, and of nights he kept up the smuggling business. And for a year or more no one knowd as it was him. But they got him at last.'

'What became of him?' We all asked it.

'He's dead,' said the old man. 'But, Lord love you, so's everybody as lived in them far-off old ancient days – all dead – Preventives too – and smugglers and gentry: all gone under the daisies.'

We felt quite sad. Oswald hastily asked if there wasn't any smuggling now.

'Not hereabouts,' the old man answered, rather quickly for him. 'Don't you go for to think it. But I did know a young chap – quite young he is with blue eyes – up Sunderland way it was. He'd got a goodish bit o' baccy and stuff done up in a ole shirt. And as he was a-goin' up off of the beach a coastguard jumps out at him, and he says to himself, "All u. p. this time," says he. But out loud he says, "Hullo, Jack, that you? I thought you was a tramp," says he.

'"What you got in that bundle?" says the coastguard.

'"My washing," says he, "and a couple of pairs of old boots."

'Then the coastguard he says, "Shall I give you a lift with it?" thinking in himself the other chap wouldn't part if it was anything it oughtn't to be. But that young chap was too sharp. He says to himself, "If I don't he'll nail me, and if I do – well, there's just a chance."

'So he hands over the bundle, and the coastguard he thinks it must be all right, and he carries it all the way up to his mother's for him, feeling sorry for the mean suspicions he'd had about the poor old chap. But that didn't happen near here. No, no.'

I think Dora was going to say, '*Old* chap – but I thought he was young with blue eyes?' but just at that minute a coastguard came along and ordered us quite harshly not to lean on the boat. He was quite disagreeable about it – how different from our own coastguards! He was from a different station to theirs. The old man got off very slowly. And all the time he was arranging his long legs so as to stand on them, the coastguard went on being disagreeable as hard as he could, in a loud voice.

When our old man had told the coastguard that no one

ever lost anything by keeping a civil tongue in his head, we all went away feeling very angry.

Alice took the old man's hand as we went back to the village, and asked him why the coastguard was so horrid.

'They gets notions into their heads,' replied the old man; 'the most innocentest people they comes to think things about. It's along of there being no smuggling in these ere parts now. The coastguards ain't got nothing to do except think things about honest people.'

We parted from the old man very warmly, all shaking hands. He lives at a cottage not quite in the village, and keeps pigs. We did not say goodbye till we had seen all the pigs.

I daresay we should not have gone on disliking that disagreeable coastguard so much if he had not come along one day when we were talking to our own coastguards, and asked why they allowed a pack of young shavers in the boat-house. We went away in silent dignity, but we did not forget, and when we were in bed that night Oswald said –

'Don't you think it would be a good thing if the coast-guards had something to do?'

Dicky yawned and said he didn't know.

'I should like to be a smuggler,' said Oswald. 'Oh, yes, go to sleep if you like; but I've got an idea, and if you'd rather be out of it I'll have Alice instead.'

'Fire away!' said Dicky, now full of attention, and leaning on his elbow.

'Well, then,' said Oswald, 'I think we *might* be smug-glers.'

'We've played all those things so jolly often,' said Dicky.

'But I don't mean play,' said Oswald. 'I mean the real thing. Of course we should have to begin in quite a small way. But we should get on in time. And we might make quite a lot for poor Miss Sandal.'

'Things that you smuggle are expensive,' said Dicky.

'Well, we've got the chink the Indian uncle sent us on Saturday. I'm certain we could do it. We'd get some one to take us out at night in one of the fishing-boats – just tear across to France and buy a keg or a bale or something, and rush back.'

'Yes, and get nabbed and put in prison. Not me,' said Dicky. 'Besides, who'd take us?'

'That old Viking man would,' said Oswald; 'but of course, if you funk it!'

'I don't funk anything,' said Dicky, 'bar making an ape of myself. Keep your hair on, Oswald. Look here. Suppose we get a keg with nothing in it – or just water. We should have all the fun, and if we *were* collared we should have the laugh of that coastguard brute.'

Oswald agreed, but he made it a condition that we should call it the keg of brandy, whatever was in it, and Dicky consented.

Smuggling is a manly sport, and girls are not fitted for it by nature. At least Dora is not; and if we had told Alice she would have insisted on dressing as a boy and going too, and we knew Father would not like this. And we thought Noël and H.O. were too young to be smugglers with any hope of success. So Dicky and I kept the idea to ourselves.

We went to see the Viking man the next day. It took us some time to make him understand what we wanted, but when he did understand he slapped his leg many times, and very hard, and declared we were chips off the old block.

'But I can't go for to let you,' he said; 'if you was nailed it's the stone jug, bless your hearts.'

So then we explained about the keg really having only water in, and he slapped his leg again harder than ever, so that it would really have been painful to any but the hardened leg of an old sea-dog. But the water made his refusals weaker, and at last he said –

'Well, see here, Benenden, him as owns the *Mary Sarah*,

he's often took out a youngster or two for the night's fishing, when their pa's and ma's hadn't no objection. You write your pa, and ask if you mayn't go for the night's fishing, or you get Mr Charteris to write. He knows it's all right, and often done by visitors' kids, if boys. And if your pa says yes, I'll make it all right with Benenden. But mind, it's just a night's fishing. No need to name no kegs. That's just betwixt ourselves.'

So we did exactly as he said. Mr Charteris is the clergyman. He was quite nice about it, and wrote for us, and Father said 'Yes, but be very careful, and don't take the girls or the little ones.'

We showed the girls the letter, and that removed the trifling ill-feeling that had grown up through Dick and me having so much secret talk about kegs and not telling the others what was up.

Of course we never breathed a word about kegs in public, and only to each other in bated breaths.

What Father said about not taking the girls or the little ones of course settled any wild ideas Alice might have had of going as a cabin-girl.

The old Viking man, now completely interested in our scheme, laid all the plans in the deepest-laid way you can think. He chose a very dark night – fortunately there was one just coming on. He chose the right time of the tide for starting, and just in the greyness of the evening when the sun is gone down, and the sea somehow looks wetter than at any other time, we put on our thick undershirts, and then our thickest suits and football jerseys over everything, because we had been told it would be very cold. Then we said goodbye to our sisters and the little ones, and it was exactly like a picture of the 'Tar's Farewell', because we had bundles, with things to eat tied up in blue checked handkerchiefs, and we said goodbye to them at the gate, and they would kiss us.

Dora said, 'Goodbye, I *know* you'll be drowned. I hope you'll enjoy yourselves, I'm sure!'

Alice said, 'I do think it's perfectly beastly. You might just as well have asked for me to go with you; or you might let us come and see you start.'

'Men must work, and women must weep,' replied Oswald with grim sadness, 'and the Viking said he wouldn't have us at all unless we could get on board in a concealed manner, like stowaways. He said a lot of others would want to go too if they saw us.'

We made our way to the beach, and we tried to conceal ourselves as much as possible, but several people did see us.

When we got to the boat we found she was manned by our Viking and Benenden, and a boy with red hair, and they were running her down to the beach on rollers. Of course Dicky and I lent a hand, shoving at the stern of the boat when the men said, 'Yo, ho! Heave ho, my merry boys all!' It wasn't exactly that that they said, but it meant the same thing, and we heaved like anything.

It was a proud moment when her nose touched the water, and prouder still when only a small part of her stern remained on the beach and Mr Benenden remarked –

'All aboard!'

The red boy gave a 'leg up' to Dicky and me and clambered up himself. Then the two men gave the last shoves to the boat, already cradled almost entirely on the bosom of the deep, and as the very end of the keel grated off the pebbles into the water, they leaped for the gunwale and hung on it with their high sea-boots waving in the evening air.

By the time they had brought their legs on board and coiled a rope or two, we chanced to look back, and already the beach seemed quite a long way off.

We were really afloat. Our smuggling expedition was no longer a dream, but a real realness. Oswald felt almost too excited at first to be able to enjoy himself. I hope you will understand this and not think the author is trying to express, by roundabout means, that the sea did not agree with Oswald. This is not the case. He was perfectly well the whole time. It was Dicky who was not. But he said it was the smell of the cabin, and not the sea, and I am sure he thought what he said was true.

In fact, that cabin was a bit stiff altogether, and was almost the means of upsetting even Oswald.

It was about six feet square, with bunks and an oil stove, and heaps of old coats and tarpaulins and sou'-westers and things, and it smelt of tar, and fish, and paraffin-smoke, and machinery oil, and of rooms where no one ever opens the window.

Oswald just put his nose in, and that was all. He had to go down later, when some fish was cooked and eaten, but by that time he had got what they call your sea-legs; but Oswald felt more as if he had got a sea-waistcoat, rather as if he had got rid of a land-waistcoat that was too heavy and too tight.

I will not weary the reader by telling about how the nets are paid out and dragged in, or about the tumbling, shining heaps of fish that come up all alive over the side of the boat, and it tips up with their weight till you think it is going over. It was a very good catch that night, and Oswald is glad he saw it, for it was very glorious. Dicky was asleep in the cabin at the time and missed it. It was deemed best not to rouse him to fresh sufferings.

It was getting latish, and Oswald, though thrilled in every marrow, was getting rather sleepy, when old Benenden said, 'There she is!'

Oswald could see nothing at first, but presently he saw a dark form on the smooth sea. It turned out to be another boat.

She crept quietly up till she was alongside ours, and then a keg was hastily hoisted from her to us.

A few words in low voices were exchanged. Oswald only heard –

'Sure you ain't give us the wrong un?'

And several people laughed hoarsely.

On first going on board Oswald and Dicky had mentioned kegs, and had been ordered to 'Stow that!' so that Oswald had begun to fear that after all it *was* only a night's fishing, and that his glorious idea had been abandoned.

But now he saw the keg his trembling heart was re-assured.

It got colder and colder. Dicky, in the cabin, was covered with several coats richly scented with fish, and Oswald was glad to accept an oilskin and sou'-wester, and to sit down on some spare nets.

Until you are out on the sea at night you can never have any idea how big the world really is. The sky looks higher up, and the stars look further off, and even if you know it is only the English Channel, yet it is just as good for feeling small on as the most trackless Atlantic or Pacific. Even the fish help to show the largeness of the world, because you think of the deep deepness of the dark sea they come up out of in such rich profusion. The hold was full of fish after the second haul.

Oswald sat leaning against the precious keg, and perhaps the bigness and quietness of everything had really rendered him unconscious. But he did not know he was asleep until the Viking man woke him up by kindly shaking him and saying –

'Here, look alive! Was ye thinking to beach her with that there precious keg of yours all above board, and crying out to be broached?'

So then Oswald roused himself, and the keg was rolled on to the fish where they lay filling the hold, and armfuls of fish thrown over it.

'Is it *really* only water?' asked Oswald. 'There's an

awfully odd smell.' And indeed, in spite of the many different smells that are natural to a fishing-boat, Oswald began to notice a strong scent of railway refreshment-rooms.

'In course it's only water,' said the Viking. 'What else would it be likely to be?' and Oswald thinks he winked in the dark.

Perhaps Oswald fell asleep again after this. It was either that or deep thought. Any way, he was aroused from it by a bump, and a soft grating sound, and he thought at first the boat was being wrecked on a coral reef or something.

But almost directly he knew that the boat had merely come ashore in the proper manner, so he jumped up.

You cannot push a boat out of the water like you push it in. It has to be hauled up by a capstan. If you don't know what that is the author is unable to explain, but there is a picture of one.

When the boat was hauled up we got out, and it was very odd to stretch your legs on land again. It felt shakier than being on sea. The red-haired boy went off to get a cart to take the shining fish to market, and Oswald decided to face the mixed-up smells of that cabin and wake Dicky.

Dicky was not grateful to Oswald for his thoughtful kindness in letting him sleep through the perils of the deep and his own uncomfortableness.

He said, 'I do think you might have waked a chap. I've simply been out of everything.'

Oswald did not answer back. His is a proud and self-restraining nature. He just said –

'Well, hurry up, now, and see them cart the fish away.'

So we hurried up, and as Oswald came out of the cabin he heard strange voices, and his heart leaped up like the persons who 'behold a rainbow in the sky,' for one of the voices was the voice of that inferior and unsailorlike coast-guard from Longbeach, who had gone out of his way to be disagreeable to Oswald and his brothers and sisters on at least two occasions. And now Oswald felt almost sure that his disagreeablenesses, though not exactly curses, were coming home to roost just as though they had been.

'You're missing your beauty sleep, Stokes,' we heard our Viking remark.

'I'm not missing anything else, though,' replied the coastguard.

'Like half a dozen mackerel for your breakfast?' inquired Mr Benenden in kindly accents.

'I've no stomach for fish, thank you all the same,' replied Mr Stokes coldly.

He walked up and down on the beach, clapping his arms to keep himself warm.

'Going to see us unload her?' asked Mr Benenden.

'If it's all the same to you,' answered the disagreeable coastguard.

He had to wait a long time, for the cart did not come, and did not come, and kept on not coming for ages and ages. When it did the men unloaded the boat, carrying the fish by basketfuls to the cart.

Every one played up jolly well. They took the fish from the side of the hold where the keg wasn't till there was quite a deep hole there, and the other side, where the keg really was, looked like a mountain in comparison.

This could be plainly seen by the detested coastguard, and by three of his companions who had now joined him.

It was beginning to be light, not daylight, but a sort of ghost-light that you could hardly believe was the beginning of sunshine, and the sky being blue again instead of black.

The hated coastguard got impatient. He said –

'You'd best own up. It'll be the better for you. It's bound to come out, along of the fish. I know it's there. We've had private information up at the station. The game's up this time, so don't you make no mistake.'

Mr Benenden and the Viking and the boy looked at each other.

'An' what might your precious private information have been about?' asked Mr Benenden.

'Brandy,' replied the coastguard Stokes, and he went and got on to the gunwale. 'And what's more, I can smell it from here.'

Oswald and Dicky drew near, and the refreshment-room smell was stronger than ever. And a brown corner of the keg was peeping out.

'There you are!' cried the Loathed One. 'Let's have that gentleman out, if you please, and then you'll all just come alonger me.'

Remarking, with a shrug of the shoulders, that he supposed it was all up, our Viking scattered the fish that hid the barrel, and hoisted it out from its scaly bed.

'That's about the size of it,' said the coastguard we did not like. 'Where's the rest?'

'That's all,' said Mr Benenden. 'We're poor men, and we has to act according to our means.'

'We'll see the boat clear to her last timber, if you've no objections,' said the Detestable One.

I could see that our gallant crew were prepared to go through with the business. More and more of the coast-guards were collecting, and I understood that what the crew wanted was to go up to the coastguard station with that keg of pretending brandy, and involve the whole of the coastguards of Longbeach in one complete and perfect sell.

But Dicky was sick of the entire business. He really has not the proper soul for adventures, and what soul he has had been damped by what he had gone through.

So he said, 'Look here, there's nothing in that keg but water.'

Oswald could have kicked him, though he is his brother.

'Huh!' replied the Unloved One, 'd'you think I haven't

got a nose? Why, it's oozing out of the bunghole now as strong as Samson.'

'Open it and see,' said Dicky, disregarding Oswald's whispered instructions to him to shut up. 'It *is* water.'

'What do you suppose I suppose you want to get water from the other side for, you young duffer!' replied the brutal official. 'There's plenty water and to spare this side.'

'It's – it's *French* water,' replied Dicky madly; 'it's ours, my brother's and mine. We asked these sailors to get it for us.'

'Sailors, indeed!' said the hateful coastguard. 'You come along with me.'

And our Viking said he was something or othered. But Benenden whispered to him in a low voice that it was all right – time was up. No one heard this but me and the Viking.

'I want to go home,' said Dicky. 'I don't want to come along with you.'

'What did you want water for?' was asked. 'To try it?'

'To stand you a drink next time you ordered us off your beastly boat,' said Dicky. And Oswald rejoiced to hear the roar of laughter that responded to this fortunate piece of cheek.

I suppose Dicky's face was so angel-like, innocent-looking, like stowaways in books, that they *had* to believe him. Oswald told him so afterwards, and Dicky hit out.

Any way, the keg was broached, and sure enough it was water, and sea-water at that, as the Unamiable One said when he had tasted it out of a tin cup, for nothing else would convince him. 'But I smell brandy still,' he said, wiping his mouth after the sea-water.

Our Viking slowly drew a good-sized flat labelled bottle out of the front of his jersey.

'From the "Old Ship",' he said gently. 'I may have spilt a drop or two here or there over the keg, my hand not being

169

very steady, as is well known, owing to spells of marsh fever as comes over me every six weeks to the day.'

The coastguard that we never could bear said, 'Marsh fever be something or othered,' and his comrades said the same. But they all blamed *him*, and we were glad.

We went home sleepy, but rejoicing. The whole thing was as complete a sell as ever I wish to see.

Of course we told our own dear and respected Lymchurch coastguards, and I think they may be trusted not to let it down on the Longbeach coastguards for many a good day. If their memories get bad I think there will always be plenty of people along that coast to remind them!

So *that's* all right.

When we had told the girls all, and borne their reproaches for not telling them before, we decided to give the Viking five bob for the game way he had played up.

So we did. He would not take it at first, but when we said, 'Do – you might buy a pig with it, and call it Stokes after that coastguard,' he could no longer resist, and accepted our friendly gift.

We talked with him for a bit, and when we were going we thanked him for being so jolly, and helping us to plant out the repulsive coastguard so thoroughly.

Then he said, 'Don't mention it. Did you tell your little gells what you was up to?'

'No,' said Oswald, 'not till afterwards.'

'Then you *can* hold your tongues. Well, since you've acted so handsome about that there pig, what's to be named for Stokes, I don't mind if I tells you something. Only mum's the word.'

We said we were quite sure it was.

'Well, then,' said he, leaning over the pigstye wall, and rubbing the spotted pig's back with his stick. 'It's an ill wind that blows no good to nobody. You see, that night there was a little bird went an whispered to 'em up at Longbeach about our little bit of a keg. So when we landed they was there.'

'Of course,' said Oswald.

'Well, if they was there they couldn't be somewheres else, could they?'

We owned they could not.

'I shouldn't wonder,' he went on, 'but what a bit of a cargo was run that night further up the beach: something as *wasn't* sea-water. I don't say it was so, mind – and mind you don't go for to say it.'

Then we understood that there is a little smuggling done still, and that we had helped in it, though quite without knowing.

We were jolly glad. Afterwards, when we had had that talk with Father, when he told us that the laws are made by the English people, and it is dishonourable for an Englishman not to stick to them, we saw that smuggling must be wrong.

But we have never been able to feel really sorry. I do not know why this is.

ZAÏDA, THE MYSTERIOUS
PROPHETESS OF THE
GOLDEN ORIENT

THIS is the story of how we were gipsies and wandering minstrels. And, like everything else we did about that time, it was done to make money for Miss Sandal, whose poorness kept on, making our kind hearts ache.

It is rather difficult to get up any good game in a house like Miss Sandal's, where there is nothing lying about, except your own things, and where everything is so neat and necessary. Your own clothes are seldom interesting, and even if you change hats with your sisters it is not a complete disguise.

The idea of being gipsies was due to Alice. She had not at all liked being entirely out of the smuggling affray, though Oswald explained to her that it was her own fault for having been born a girl. And, of course, after the event, Dicky and I had some things to talk about that the girls hadn't, and we had a couple of wet days.

You have no idea how dull you can be in a house like that, unless you happen to know the sort of house I mean. A house that is meant for plain living and high thinking, like Miss Sandal told us, may be very nice for the high thinkers, but if you are not accustomed to thinking high there is only the plain living left, and it is like boiled rice for every meal to any young mind, however much beef and Yorkshire there may be for the young insides. Mrs Beale saw to our having plenty of nice things to eat, but, alas! it is not always dinner-time, and in between meals the cold rice-pudding feeling is very chilling. Of course we had the splendid drawings of winged things made by our Flying Lodger, but you cannot look at pictures all day long, however many coloured chalks they are drawn with, and however fond you may be of them.

Miss Sandal's was the kind of house that makes you wander all round it and say, 'What shall we do next?' And when it rains the little ones get cross.

It was the second wet day when we were wandering round the house to the sad music of our boots on the clean, bare boards that Alice said –

'Mrs Beale has got a book at her house called *Napoleon's Book of Fate*. You might ask her to let you go and get it, Oswald. She likes you best.'

Oswald is as modest as any one I know, but the truth is the truth.

'We could tell our fortunes, and read the dark future,' Alice went on. 'It would be better than high thinking without anything particular to think about.'

So Oswald went down to Mrs Beale and said –

'I say, Bealie dear, you've got a book up at your place. I wish you'd lend it to us to read.'

'If it's the Holy Book you mean, sir,' replied Mrs Beale, going on with peeling the potatoes that were to be a radiant vision later on, all brown and crisp in company with a leg of mutton – 'if it's the Holy Book you want there's one up on Miss Sandal's chest of drawerses.'

'I know,' said Oswald. He knew every book in the house. The backs of them were beautiful – leather and gold – but inside they were like whited sepulchres, full of poetry and improving reading. 'No – we didn't want that book just now. It is a book called *Napoleon's Book of Fate*. Would you mind if I ran up to your place and got it?'

'There's no one at home,' said Mrs Beale; 'wait a bit till I go along to the bakus with the meat, and I'll fetch it along.'

'You might let me go,' said Oswald, whose high spirit is

always ill-attuned to waiting a bit. 'I wouldn't touch anything else, and I know where you keep the key.'

'There's precious little as ye don't know, it seems to me,' said Mrs Beale. 'There, run along do. It's on top of the mantelshelf alongside the picture tea-tin. It's a red book. Don't go taking the *Wesleyan Conference Reports* by mistake, the two is both together on the mantel.'

Oswald in his macker splashed through the mud to Mrs Beale's, found the key under the loose tile behind the water-butt, and got the book without adventure. He had promised not to touch anything else, so he could not make even the gentlest booby-trap as a little surprise for Mrs Beale when she got back.

And most of that day we were telling our fortunes by the ingenious means invented by the great Emperor, or by cards, which it is hard to remember the rules for, or by our dreams. The only blights were that the others all wanted to have the book all the time, and that Noël's dreams were so long and mixed that we got tired of hearing about them before he did. But he said he was quite sure he had dreamed every single bit of every one of them. And the author hopes this was the truth.

We all went to bed hoping we should dream something that we could look up in the dream book, but none of us did.

And in the morning it was still raining and Alice said –

'Look here, if it ever clears up again let's dress up and be gipsies. We can go about in the distant villages telling people's fortunes. If you'll let me have the book all to-day I can learn up quite enough to tell them mysteriously and darkly. And gipsies always get their hands crossed with silver.'

Dicky said that was one way of keeping the book to herself, but Oswald said –

'Let us try. She shall have it for an hour, and then we'll have an exam. to see how much she knows.'

This was done, but while she was swatting the thing up with her fingers in her ears we began to talk about how gipsies should be dressed.

And when we all went out of the room to see if we could find anything in that tidy house to dress up in, she came after us to see what was up. So there was no exam.

We peeped into the cupboards and drawers in Miss Sandal's room, but everything was grey or brown, not at all the sort of thing to dress up for children of the Sunny South in. The plain living was shown in all her clothes; and besides, grey shows every little spot you may happen to get on it.

We were almost in despair. We looked in all the drawers in all the rooms, but found only sheets and tablecloths and more grey and brown clothing.

We tried the attic, with fainting hearts. Servants' clothes are always good for dressing-up with; they have so many different colours. But Miss Sandal had no servant. Still, she might have had one once, and the servant might have left something behind her. Dora suggested this and added –

'If you don't find anything in the attic you'll know it's Fate, and you're not to do it. Besides, I'm almost sure you can be put in prison for telling fortunes.'

'Not if you're a gipsy you can't,' said Noël; 'they have licences to tell fortunes, I believe, and judges can't do anything to them.'

So we went up to the attic. And it was as bare and tidy as the rest of the house. But there were some boxes and we looked in them. The smallest was full of old letters, so we shut it again at once. Another had books in it, and the last had a clean towel spread over what was inside. So we took off the towel, and then every one said 'Oh!'

In right on the top was a scarlet thing, embroidered heavily with gold. It proved, on unfolding, to be a sort of coat, like a Chinaman's. We lifted it out and laid it on the towel on the floor. And then the full glories of that box were revealed. There were cloaks and dresses and skirts and scarves, of all the colours of a well-chosen rainbow, and all made of the most beautiful silks and stuffs, with things worked on them with silk, as well as chains of beads and many lovely ornaments. We think Miss Sandal must have been very fond of pretty things when she was young, or when she was better off.

'Well, there won't be any gipsies near by to come up to *us*,' said Oswald joyously.

'Do you think we ought to take them, without asking?' said Dora.

'Of course not,' said Oswald witheringly; 'we ought to write to her and say, "Please, Miss Sandal, we know how poor you are, and may we borrow your things to be gipsies in so as we got money for you —" All right! You go and write the letter, Dora.'

'I only just asked,' said Dora.

We tried the things on. Some of them were so ladylike that they were no good – evening dresses, and things like that. But there were enough useful things to go round. Oswald, in white shirt and flannel knee-breeches, tied a brick-coloured silk scarf round his middle part, and a green one round his head for a turban. The turban was fastened with a sparkling brooch with pink stones in it. He looked like a Moorish toreador. Dicky had the scarlet and gold coat, which was the right length when Dora had run a tuck in it.

Alice had a blue skirt with embroidery of peacock's feathers on it, and a gold and black jacket very short with no sleeves, and a yellow silk handkerchief on her head like Italian peasants, and another handkie round her neck. Dora's skirt was green and her handkerchiefs purple and pink.

Noël insisted on having his two scarves, one green and

one yellow, twisted on his legs like putties, and a red scarf wound round his middle-part, and he stuck a long ostrich feather in his own bicycle cap and said he was a troubadour bard.

H.O. was able to wear a lady's blouse of mouse-coloured silk, embroidered with poppies. It came down to his knees and a jewelled belt kept it in place.

We made up our costumes into bundles, and Alice thoughtfully bought a pennyworth of pins. Of course it was idle to suppose that we could go through the village in our gipsy clothes without exciting *some* remark.

The more we thought of it the more it seemed as if it would be a good thing to get some way from our village before we began our gipsy career.

The woman at the sweet shop where Alice got the pins has a donkey and cart, and for two shillings she consented to lend us this, so that some of us could walk while some of us would always be resting in the cart.

And next morning the weather was bright and blue as ever, and we started. We were beautifully clean, but all our hairs had been arranged with a brush solely, because at the last moment nobody could find its comb. Mrs Beale had packed up a jolly sandwichy and apply lunch for us. We told her we were going to gather bluebells in the woods, and of course we meant to do that too.

The donkey-cart drew up at the door and we started. It was found impossible to get every one into the cart at once, so we agreed to cast lots for who should run behind, and to take it in turns, mile and mile. The lot fell on Dora and H.O., but there was precious little running about. Anything slower than that donkey Oswald has never known, and when it came to passing its own front door the donkey simply would not. It ended in Oswald getting down and going to the animal's head, and having it out with him, man to man. The donkey was small, but of enormous strength.

He set all his four feet firm and leant back – and Oswald set his two feet firm and leant back – so that Oswald and the front part of the donkey formed an angry and contentious letter V. And Oswald gazed in the donkey's eyes in a dauntless manner, and the donkey looked at Oswald as though it thought he was hay or thistles.

Alice beat the donkey from the cart with a stick that had been given us for the purpose. The rest shouted. But all was in vain. And four people in a motor car stopped it to see the heroic struggle, and laughed till I thought they would have upset their hateful motor. However, it was all for the best, though Oswald did not see it at the time. When they had had enough of laughing they started their machine again, and the noise it made penetrated the donkey's dull intelligence, and he started off without a word – I mean without any warning, and Oswald had only just time to throw himself clear of the wheels before he fell on the ground and rolled over, biting the dust.

The motor car people behaved as you would expect. But accidents happen even to motor cars, when people laugh too long and too unfeelingly. The driver turned round to laugh, and the motor instantly took the bit between its teeth and bolted into the stone wall of the churchyard. No one was hurt except the motor, but that had to spend the day at the blacksmith's, we heard afterwards. Thus was the outraged Oswald avenged by Fate.

He was not hurt either – though much the motor people would have cared if he had been – and he caught up with the others at the end of the village, for the donkey's pace had been too good to last, and the triumphal progress was resumed.

It was some time before we found a wood sufficiently lurking-looking for our secret purposes. There are no woods close to the village. But at last, up by Bonnington, we found one, and tying our noble steed to the sign-post that says how many miles it is to Ashford, we cast a hasty glance round, and finding no one in sight disappeared in the wood with our bundles.

We went in just ordinary creatures. We came out gipsies of the deepest dye, for we had got a pennorth of walnut stain from Mr Jameson the builder, and mixed with water – the water we had brought in a medicine-bottle – it was a prime disguise. And we knew it would wash off, unlike the Condy's fluid we once stained ourselves with during a never-to-be-forgotten game of Jungle-Book.

We had put on all the glorious things we had bagged from Miss Sandal's attic treasures, but still Alice had a small bundle unopened.

'What's that?' Dora asked.

'I meant to keep it as a reserve force in case the fortune-telling didn't turn out all our fancy painted it,' said Alice; 'but I don't mind telling you now.'

She opened the bundle, and there was a tambourine, some black lace, a packet of cigarette papers, and our missing combs.

'What ever on earth –' Dicky was beginning, but Oswald saw it all. He has a wonderfully keen nose. And he said –

'Bully for you, Alice. I wish I'd thought it myself.'

Alice was much pleased by this handsome speech.

'Yes,' she said; 'perhaps really it would be best to begin with it. It would attract the public's attention, and then we could tell the fortunes. You see,' she kindly explained to Dicky and H.O. and Dora, who had not seen it yet – though Noël had, almost as soon as I did – 'you see, we'll all play on the combs with the veils over our faces, so that no one can see what our instruments are. Why, they might be mouth-organs for anything any one will know, or some costly instruments from the far-off East, like they play to sultans in zenanas. Let's just try a tune or two before we go on, to be sure that all the combs work right. Dora's has such big teeth, I shouldn't wonder if it wouldn't act at all.'

So we all papered our combs and did 'Heroes', but that sounded awful. 'The Girl I Left Behind Me' went better, and so did 'Bonnie Dundee'. But we thought 'See the Conquering' or 'The Death of Nelson' would be the best to begin with.

It was beastly hot doing it under the veils, but when Oswald had done one tune without the veil to see how the others looked he could not help owning that the veils did give a hidden mystery that was a stranger to simple combs.

We were all a bit puffed when we had played for a while, so we decided that as the donkey seemed calm and was eating grass and resting, we might as well follow his example.

'We ought not to be too proud to take pattern by the brute creation,' said Dora.

So we had our lunch in the wood. We lighted a little fire of sticks and fir-cones, so as to be as gipsyish as we could, and we sat round the fire. We made a charming picture in our bright clothes, among what would have been our native surroundings if we had been real gipsies, and we knew how nice we looked, and stayed there though the smoke got in our eyes, and everything we ate tasted of it.

The woods were a little damp, and that was why the fire smoked so. There were the jackets we had cast off when we dressed up, to sit on, and there was a horse-cloth in the cart intended for the donkey's wear, but we decided that our need was greater than its, so we took the blanket to recline on.

It was as jolly a lunch as ever I remember, and we lingered over that and looking romantic till we could not bear the smoke any more.

Then we got a lot of bluebells and we trampled out the fire most carefully, because we know about not setting woods and places alight, rolled up our clothes in bundles, and went out of the shadowy woodland into the bright sunlight, as sparkling looking a crew of gipsies as any one need wish for.

Last time we had seen the road it had been quite white and bare of persons walking on it, but now there were several. And not only walkers, but people in carts. And some carriages passed us too.

Every one stared at us, but they did not seem so astonished as we had every right to expect, and though interested they were not rude, and this is very rare among English people – and not only poor people either – when they see anything at all out of the way.

We asked one man, who was very Sunday-best indeed in black clothes and a blue tie, where every one was going, for every one was going the same way, and every one looked as if it was going to church, which was unlikely, it being but Thursday. He said –

'Same place wot you're going to I expect.'

And when we said where was that we were requested by him to get along with us. Which we did.

An old woman in the heaviest bonnet I have ever seen and the highest – it was like a black church – revealed the secret to us, and we learned that there was a Primrose *fête* going on in Sir Willoughby Blockson's grounds.

We instantly decided to go to the *fête*.

'I've been to a Primrose *fête*, and so have you, Dora,' Oswald remarked, 'and people are so dull at them, they'd gladly give gold to see the dark future. And, besides, the villages will be unpopulated, and no one at home but idiots and babies and their keepers.'

So we went to the *fête*.

The people got thicker and thicker, and when we got to Sir Willoughby's lodge gates, which have sprawling lions on the gate-posts, we were told to take the donkey-cart round to the stable-yard.

This we did, and proud was the moment when a stiff groom had to bend his proud stomach to go to the head of Bates's donkey.

'This is something like,' said Alice, and Noël added:

'The foreign princes are well received at this palace.'

'We aren't princes, we're gipsies,' said Dora, tucking his scarf in. It would keep on getting loose.

'There *are* gipsy princes, though,' said Noël, 'because there are gipsy kings.'

'You aren't always a prince first,' said Dora; 'don't wriggle so or I can't fix you. Sometimes being made a king just happens to some one who isn't any one in particular.'

'I don't think so,' said Noël; 'you have to be a prince before you're a king, just as you have to be a kitten before you're a cat, or a puppy before you're a dog, or a worm before you're a serpent, or –'

'What about the King of Sweden?' Dora was beginning, when a very nice tall, thin man, with white flowers in his buttonhole like for a wedding, came strolling up and said –

'And whose show is this? Eh, what?'

We said it was ours.

'Are you expected?' he asked.

We said we thought not, but we hoped he didn't mind.

'What are you? Acrobats? Tight-rope? That's a ripping Burmese coat you've got there.'

'Yes, it is. No we aren't,' said Alice, with dignity. 'I am Zaïda, the mysterious prophetess of the golden Orient, and the others are mysterious too, but we haven't fixed on their names yet.'

'By Jove!' said the gentleman; 'but who are you really?'

'Our names are our secret,' said Oswald, with dignity, but Alice said, 'Oh, but we don't mind telling *you*, because I'm sure you're nice. We're really the Bastables, and we want to get some money for some one we know that's rather poor – of course I can't tell you *her* name. And we've learnt how to tell fortunes – really we have. Do you think they'll let us tell them at the *fête*. People are often dull at *fêtes*, aren't they?'

'By Jove!' said the gentleman again – 'by Jove, they are!'

He plunged for a moment in deep reflection.

'We've got co— musical instruments,' said Noël; 'shall we play to you a little?'

'Not here,' said the gentleman; 'follow me.'

He led the way by the backs of shrubberies to an old summer-house, and we asked him to wait outside.

Then we put on our veils and tuned up. 'See, see the conquering –'

But he did not let us finish the tune; he burst in upon us, crying –

'Ripping – oh, ripping! And now tell me my fortune.'

Alice took off her veil and looked at his hand.

'You will travel in distant lands,' she said; 'you will have great wealth and honour; you will marry a beautiful lady – a very fine woman, it says in the book, but I think a beautiful lady sounds nicer, don't you?'

'Much; but I shouldn't mention the book when you're telling the fortune.'

'I wouldn't, except to you,' said Alice, 'and she'll have lots of money and a very sweet disposition. Trials and troubles beset your path, but do but be brave and fearless and you will overcome all your enemies. Beware of a dark woman – most likely a widow.'

'I will,' said he, for Alice had stopped for breath. 'Is that all?'

'No. Beware of a dark woman and shun the society of drunkards and gamblers. Be very cautious in your choice of acquaintances, or you will make a false friend who will be your ruin. That's all, except that you will be married very soon and live to a green old age with the beloved wife of your bosom, and have twelve sons and –'

'Stop, stop!' said the gentleman; 'twelve sons are as many as I can bring up handsomely on my present income. Now, look here. You did that jolly well, only go slower, and pretend to look for things in the hand before you say them. Everything's free at the *fête*, so you'll get no money for your fortune-telling.'

Gloom was on each young brow.

'It's like this,' he went on, 'there is a lady fortune-teller in a tent in the park.'

'Then we may as well get along home,' said Dicky.

'Not at all,' said our new friend, for such he was now about to prove himself to be; 'that lady does not want to tell fortunes to-day. She has a headache. Now, if you'll really stick to it, and tell the people's fortunes as well as you told mine, I'll stand you – let's see – two quid for the afternoon. Will that do? What?'

We said we should just jolly well think it would.

'I've got some Eau de Cologne in a medicine-bottle,' Dora said; 'my brother Noël has headaches sometimes, but I think he's going to be all right to-day. Do take it, it will do the lady's head good.'

'I'll take care of her head,' he said, laughing, but he took the bottle and said, 'Thank you.'

Then he told us to stay where we were while he made final arrangements, and we were left with palpitating breasts to look wildly through the Book of Fate, so as to have the things ready. But it turned out to be time thrown away, for when he came back he said to Alice –

'It'll have to be only you and your sister, please, for I see they've stuck up a card with "Esmeralda, the gipsy Princess, reads the hand and foretells the future" on it. So you boys will have to be mum. You can be attendants – mutes, by Jove! – yes that's it. And, I say, kiddies, you will jolly well play up, won't you? Don't stand any cheek. Stick it on, you know. I can't tell you how important it is about – about the lady's headache.'

'I should think this would be a cool place for a headache to be quiet in,' said Dora; and it was, for it was quite hidden in the shrubbery and no path to it.

'By Jove!' he remarked yet once again, 'so it would. You're right!'

He led us out of the shrubbery and across the park. There were people dotted all about and they stared, but they touched their hats to the gentleman, and he returned their salute with stern politeness.

Inside the tent with 'Esmeralda, &c.', outside there was a lady in a hat and dust-cloak. But we could see her spangles under the cloak.

'Now,' said the gentleman to Dicky, 'you stand at the door and let people in, one at a time. You others can just play a few bars on your instruments for each new person – only a very little, because you do get out of tune, though that's barbaric certainly. Now, here's the two quid. And you stick to the show till five; you'll hear the stable clock chime.'

The lady was very pale with black marks under her eyes, and her eyes looked red, Oswald thought. She seemed about to speak, but the gentleman said –

'Do trust me, Ella. I'll explain everything directly. Just go to the old summer-house – *you* know – and I'll be there directly. I'll take a couple of pegs out of the back and you can slip away among the trees. Hold your cloak close over your gown. Goodbye, kiddies. Stay, give me your address, and I'll write and tell you if my fortune comes true.'

So he shook hands with us and went. And we did stick to it, though it is far less fun than you would think telling fortunes all the afternoon in a stuffy tent, while outside you know there are things to eat and people enjoying themselves. But there were the two gold quid, and we were determined to earn them. It is very hard to tell a different fortune for each person, and there were a great many. The girls took it in turns, and Oswald wonders why their hairs did not go grey. Though of course it was much better fun for them than for us, because we had just to be mutes when we weren't playing on the combs.

The people we told fortunes to at first laughed rather, and said we were too young to know anything. But Oswald said in a hollow voice that we were as old as the Pyramids, and after that Alice took the tucks out of Dicky's red coat and put it on and turbaned herself, and looked much older.

The stable clock had chimed the quarter to five some little time, when an elderly gentleman with whiskers, who afterwards proved to be Sir Willoughby, burst into the tent.

'Where's Miss Blockson?' he said, and we answered truthfully that we did not know.

'How long have you been here?' he furiously asked.

'Ever since two,' said Alice wearily.

He said a word that I should have thought a baronet would have been above using.

'Who brought you here?'

We described the gentleman who had done this, and again the baronet said things we should never be allowed to say. 'That confounded Carew!' he added, with more words.

'Is anything wrong?' asked Dora – 'can we do anything? We'll stay on longer if you like – if you can't find the lady who was doing Esmeralda before we came.'

'I'm not very likely to find her,' he said ferociously. 'Stay longer indeed! Get away out of my sight before I have you locked up for vagrants and vagabonds.'

He left the scene in bounding and mad fury. We thought it best to do as he said, and went round the back way to the stables so as to avoid exciting his ungoverned rage by meeting him again. We found our cart and went home. We had got two quid and something to talk about.

But none of us – not even Oswald the discerning – understood exactly what we had been mixed up in, till the pink satin box with three large bottles of A1 scent in it, and postmarks of foreign lands, came to Dora. And there was a letter. It said –

MY DEAR GIPSIES, – I beg to return the Eau de Cologne you so kindly lent me. The lady did use a little of it, but I found that foreign travel was what she really wanted to make her quite happy. So we caught the 4.15 to town, and now we are married, and intend to live to a green old age, &c., as you foretold. But for your help my fortune couldn't have come true, because my wife's father, Sir Willoughby, thought I was not rich enough to marry. But you see I was. And my wife and I both thank you heartily for your kind help. I hope it was not an awful swat. I had to say five because of the train. Good luck to you, and thanks awfully.

Yours faithfully,
CARISBROOK CAREW.

If Oswald had known beforehand we should never have made that two quid for Miss Sandal.

For Oswald does not approve of marriages and would never, if he knew it, be the means of assisting one to occur.

THE LADY AND THE LICENCE;
OR, FRIENDSHIP'S GARLAND

MY DEAR KIDDIES, – Miss Sandal's married sister has just come home from Australia, and she feels very tired. No wonder, you will say, after such a long journey. So she is going to Lymchurch to rest. Now I want you all to be very quiet, because when you are in your usual form you aren't exactly restful, are you? If this weather lasts you will be able to be out most of the time, and when you are indoors for goodness' sake control your lungs and your boots, especially H.O.'s. Mrs Bax has travelled about a good deal, and once was nearly eaten by cannibals. But I hope you won't bother her to tell you stories. She is coming on Friday. I am glad to hear from Alice's letter that you enjoyed the Primrose Fête. Tell Noël that 'poetticle' is not the usual way of spelling the word he wants. I send you ten shillings for pocket-money, and again implore you to let Mrs Bax have a little rest and peace.

Your loving
FATHER.

PS. If you want anything sent down, tell me, and I will get Mrs Bax to bring it. I met your friend Mr Red House the other day at lunch.

When the letter had been read aloud, and we had each read it to ourselves, a sad silence took place.

Dicky was the first to speak.

'It *is* rather beastly, I grant you,' he said, 'but it might be worse.'

'I don't see how,' said H.O. 'I do wish Father would jolly well learn to leave my boots alone.'

'It might be worse, I tell you,' said Dicky. 'Suppose

instead of telling us to keep out of doors it had been the other way?'

'Yes,' said Alice, 'suppose it had been, "Poor Mrs Bax requires to be cheered up. Do not leave her side day or night. Take it in turns to make jokes for her. Let not a moment pass without some merry jest"? Oh yes, it might be much, much worse.'

'Being able to get out all day makes it all right about trying to make that two pounds increase and multiply,' remarked Oswald. 'Now who's going to meet her at the station? Because after all it's her sister's house, and we've got to be polite to visitors even if we're in a house we aren't related to.'

This was seen to be so, but no one was keen on going to the station. At last Oswald, ever ready for forlorn hopes, consented to go.

We told Mrs Beale, and she got the best room ready, scrubbing everything till it smelt deliciously of wet wood and mottled soap. And then we decorated the room as well as we could.

'She'll want some pretty things,' said Alice, 'coming from the land of parrots and opossums and gum-trees and things.'

We did think of borrowing the stuffed wild-cat that is in the bar at the 'Ship', but we decided that our decorations must be very quiet – and the wild-cat, even in its stuffed state, was anything but; so we borrowed a stuffed roach in a glass box and stood it on the chest of drawers. It looked very calm. Sea-shells are quiet things when they are vacant, and Mrs Beale let us have the four big ones off her chiffonnier.

The girls got flowers – bluebells and white wood-anemones. We might have had poppies or buttercups, but we thought the colours might be too loud. We took some books up for Mrs Bax to read in the night. And we took the quietest ones we could find.

Sonnets on Sleep, Confessions of an Opium Eater, Twilight of the Gods, Diary of a Dreamer, and *By Still Walters,* were some of them. The girls covered them with grey paper, because some of the bindings were rather gay.

The girls hemmed grey calico covers for the drawers and the dressing-table, and we drew the blinds half-down, and when all was done the room looked as quiet as a roosting wood-pigeon.

We put in a clock, but we did not wind it up.

'She can do that herself,' said Dora, 'if she feels she can bear to hear it ticking.'

Oswald went to the station to meet her. He rode on the box beside the driver. When the others saw him mount there I think they were sorry they had not been polite and gone to meet her themselves. Oswald had a jolly ride. We got to the station just as the train came in. Only one lady got out of it, so Oswald knew it must be Mrs Bax. If he had not been told how quiet she wanted to be he would have thought she looked rather jolly. She had short hair and gold spectacles. Her skirts were short, and she carried a parrot-cage in her hand. It contained our parrot, and when we wrote to tell Father that it and Pincher were the only things we wanted sent we never thought she would have brought either.

'Mrs Bax, I believe,' was the only break Oswald made in the polite silence that he took the parrot-cage and her bag from her in.

'How do you do?' she said very briskly for a tired lady; and Oswald thought it was noble of her to make the effort to smile. 'Are you Oswald or Dicky?'

Oswald told her in one calm word which he was, and then Pincher rolled madly out of a dog-box almost into his arms. Pincher would not be quiet. Of course he did not understand the need for it. Oswald conversed with Pincher in low, restraining whispers as he led the way to the 'Ship's' fly. He put the parrot-cage on the inside seat of the carriage, held the door open for Mrs Bax with silent politeness, closed it as quietly as possible, and prepared to mount on the box.

'Oh, won't you come inside?' asked Mrs Bax. 'Do!'

'No, thank you,' said Oswald in calm and mouse-like tones; and to avoid any more jaw he got at once on to the box with Pincher.

So that Mrs Bax was perfectly quiet for the whole six miles – unless you count the rattle and shake-up-and-down of the fly. On the box Oswald and Pincher 'tasted the sweets of a blissful re-union', like it says in novels. And the man from the 'Ship' looked on and said how well bred Pincher was. It was a happy drive.

There was something almost awful about the sleek, quiet tidiness of the others, who were all standing in a row outside the cottage to welcome Mrs Bax. They all said, 'How do you do?' in hushed voices, and all looked as if butter would not melt in any of their young mouths. I never saw a more soothing-looking lot of kids.

She went to her room, and we did not see her again till tea-time.

Then, still exquisitely brushed and combed, we sat round the board – in silence. We had left the tea-tray place for Mrs Bax, of course. But she said to Dora –

'Wouldn't you like to pour out?'

And Dora replied in low, soft tones, 'If you wish me to, Mrs Bax. I usually do.' And she did.

We passed each other bread-and-butter and jam and honey with silent courteousness. And of course we saw that she had enough to eat.

'Do you manage to amuse yourself pretty well here?' she asked presently.

We said, 'Yes, thank you,' in hushed tones.

'What do you do?' she asked.

We did not wish to excite her by telling her what we did, so Dicky murmured –

'Nothing in particular,' at the same moment that Alice said –

'All sorts of things.'

'Tell me about them,' said Mrs Bax invitingly.

We replied by a deep silence. She sighed, and passed her cup for more tea.

'Do you ever feel shy,' she asked suddenly. 'I do, dreadfully, with new people.'

We liked her for saying that, and Alice replied that she hoped she would not feel shy with us.

'I hope not,' she said. 'Do you know, there was such a funny woman in the train? She had seventeen different parcels, and she kept counting them, and one of them was a kitten, and it was always under the seat when she began to count, so she always got the number wrong.'

We should have liked to hear about that kitten – especially what colour it was and how old – but Oswald felt that Mrs Bax was only trying to talk for our sakes, so that we shouldn't feel shy, so he simply said, 'Will you have some more cake?' and nothing more was said about the kitten.

Mrs Bax seemed very noble. She kept trying to talk to us about Pincher, and trains and Australia, but we were determined she should be quiet, as she wished it so much, and we restrained our brimming curiosity about opossums up gum-trees, and about emus and kangaroos and wattles, and only said 'Yes' or 'No', or, more often, nothing at all.

When tea was over we melted away, 'like snow-wreaths in Thawjean,' and went out on the beach and had a yelling match. Our throats felt as though they were full of wool, from the hushed tones we had used in talking to Mrs Bax. Oswald won the match. Next day we kept carefully out of the way, except for meals. Mrs Bax tried talking again at breakfast-time, but we checked our wish to listen, and passed the pepper, salt, mustard, bread, toast, butter, marmalade, and even the cayenne, vinegar, and oil, with such politeness that she gave up.

We took it in turns to watch the house and drive away organ-grinders. We told them they must not play in front of that house, because there was an Australian lady who had to be kept quiet. And they went at once. This cost us expense, because an organ-grinder will never consent to fly the spot under twopence a flight.

We went to bed early. We were quite weary with being so calm and still. But we knew it was our duty, and we liked the feel of having done it.

The day after was the day Jake Lee got hurt. Jake is the man who drives about the country in a covered cart, with pins and needles, and combs and frying-pans, and all the sort of things that farmers' wives are likely to want in a hurry, and no shops for miles. I have always thought Jake's was a beautiful life. I should like to do it myself. Well, this particular day he had got his cart all ready to start and had got his foot on the wheel to get up, when a motor-car went by puffing and hooting. I always think motor-cars seem so rude somehow. And the horse was frightened; and no wonder. It shied, and poor Jake was thrown violently to the ground, and hurt so much that they had to send for the doctor. Of course we went and asked Mrs Jake if we could do anything – such as take the cart out and sell the things to the farmers' wives.

But she thought not.

It was after this that Dicky said –

'Why shouldn't we get things of our own and go and sell them – with Bates' donkey?'

Oswald was thinking the same thing, but he wishes to be fair, so he owns that Dicky spoke first. We all saw at once that the idea was a good one.

'Shall we dress up for it?' H.O. asked. We thought not. It

is always good sport to dress up, but I have never heard of people selling things to farmers' wives in really beautiful disguises.

'We ought to go as shabby as we can,' said Alice; 'but somehow that always seems to come natural to your clothes when you've done a few interesting things in them. We have plenty of clothes that look poor but deserving. What shall we buy to sell?'

'Pins and needles, and tape and bodkins,' said Dora.

'Butter,' said Noël; 'it is terrible when there is no butter.'

'Honey is nice,' said H.O., 'and so are sausages.'

'Jake has ready-made shirts and corduroy trousers. I suppose a farmer's shirt and trousers may give at any moment,' said Alice, 'and if he can't get new ones he has to go to bed till they are mended.'

Oswald thought tin-tacks, and glue, and string must often be needed to mend barns and farm tools with if they broke suddenly. And Dicky said –

'I think the pictures of ladies hanging on to crosses in foaming seas are good. Jake told me he sold more of them than anything. I suppose people suddenly break the old ones, and home isn't home without a lady holding on to a cross.'

We went to Munn's shop, and we bought needles and pins, and tapes and bodkins, a pound of butter, a pot of honey and one of marmalade, and tin-tacks, string, and glue. But we could not get any ladies with crosses, and the shirts and trousers were too expensive for us to dare to risk it. Instead, we bought a head-stall for eighteenpence, because how providential we should be to a farmer whose favourite horse had escaped and he had nothing to catch it with; and three tin-openers, in case of a distant farm subsisting entirely on tinned things, and the only opener for miles lost down the well or something. We also bought several other thoughtful and far-sighted things.

That night at supper we told Mrs Bax we wanted to go out for the day. She had hardly said anything that supper-time, and now she said –

'Where are you going? Teaching Sunday school?'

As it was Monday, we felt her poor brain was wandering – most likely for want of quiet. And the room smelt of tobacco smoke, so we thought some one had been to see her and perhaps been too noisy for her. So Oswald said gently –

'No, we are not going to teach Sunday school.'

Mrs Bax sighed. Then she said –

'I am going out myself to-morrow – for the day.'

'I hope it will not tire you too much,' said Dora, with soft-voiced and cautious politeness. 'If you want anything bought we could do it for you, with pleasure, and you could have a nice, quiet day at home.'

'Thank you,' said Mrs Bax shortly; and we saw she would do what she chose, whether it was really for her own good or not.

She started before we did next morning, and we were careful to be mouse-quiet till the 'Ship's' fly which contained her was out of hearing. Then we had another yelling competition, and Noël won with that new shriek of his that is like railway engines in distress; and then we went and fetched Bates' donkey and cart and packed our bales in it and started, some riding and some running behind.

Any faint distant traces of respectableness that were left to our clothes were soon covered up by the dust of the road and by some of the ginger-beer bursting through the violence of the cart, which had no springs.

The first farm we stopped at the woman really did want some pins, for though a very stupid person, she was making a pink blouse, and we said –

'Do have some tape! You never know when you may want it.'

'I believe in buttons,' she said. 'No strings for me, thank you.'

But when Oswald said, 'What about pudding-strings? You can't button up puddings as if they were pillows!' she consented to listen to reason. But it was only twopence altogether.

But at the next place the woman said we were 'mummickers', and told us to 'get along, do'. And she set her dog at us; but when Pincher sprang from the inmost recesses of the cart she called her dog off. But too late, for it and Pincher were locked in the barking, scuffling, growling embrace of deadly combat. When we had separated the dogs she went into her house and banged the door, and we went on through the green flat marshes, among the buttercups and may-bushes.

'I wonder what she meant by "mummickers"?' said H.O.

'She meant she saw our high-born airs through our shabby clothes,' said Alice. 'It's always happening, especially to princes. There's nothing so hard to conceal as a really high-bred air.'

'I've been thinking,' said Dicky, 'whether honesty wouldn't perhaps be the best policy – not always, of course; but just this once. If people knew what we were doing it for they might be glad to help on the good work – What?'

So at the next farm, which was half hidden by trees, like the picture at the beginning of *Sensible Susan*, we tied the pony to the gate-post and knocked at the door. It was opened by a man this time, and Dora said to him –

'We are honest traders. We are trying to sell these things to keep a lady who is poor. If you buy some you will be helping too. Wouldn't you like to do that? It is a good work, and you will be glad of it afterwards, when you come to think over the acts of your life.'

'Upon my word an' 'onner!' said the man, whose red face

was surrounded by a frill of white whiskers. 'If ever I see a walkin' Tract 'ere it stands!'

'She doesn't mean to be tractish,' said Oswald quickly; 'it's only her way. But we really are trying to sell things to help a poor person – no humbug, sir – so if we *have* got anything you want we shall be glad. And if not – well, there's no harm in asking, is there, sir?'

The man with the frilly whiskers was very pleased to be called 'sir' – Oswald knew he would be – and he looked at everything we'd got, and bought the head-stall and two tin-openers, and a pot of marmalade, and a ball of string, and a pair of braces. This came to four and twopence, and we were very pleased. It really seemed that our business was establishing itself root and branch.

When it came to its being dinner-time, which was first noticed through H.O. beginning to cry and say he did not want to play any more, it was found that we had forgotten to bring any dinner. So we had to eat some of our stock – the jam, the biscuits, and the cucumber.

'I feel a new man,' said Alice, draining the last of the ginger-beer bottles. 'At that homely village on the brow of yonder hill we shall sell all that remains of the stock, and go home with money in both pockets.'

But our luck had changed. As so often happens, our hearts beat high with hopeful thoughts, and we felt jollier than we had done all day. Merry laughter and snatches of musical song re-echoed from our cart, and from round it as we went up the hill. All Nature was smiling and gay. There was nothing sinister in the look of the trees or the road – or anything.

Dogs are said to have inside instincts that warn them of intending perils, but Pincher was not a bit instinctive that day somehow. He sported gaily up and down the hedge-banks after pretending rats, and once he was so excited that I believe he was playing at weasels and stoats. But of course there was really no trace of these savage denizens of the jungle. It was just Pincher's varied imagination.

We got to the village, and with joyful expectations we knocked at the first door we came to.

Alice had spread out a few choice treasures – needles, pins, tape, a photograph-frame, and the butter, rather soft by now, and the last of the tin-openers – on a basket-lid, like the fish-man does with herrings and whitings and plums and apples (you cannot sell fish in the country unless you sell fruit too. The author does not know why this is).

The sun was shining, the sky was blue. There was no sign at all of the intending thunderbolt, not even when the door was opened. This was done by a woman.

She just looked at our basket-lid of things any one might have been proud to buy, and smiled. I saw her do it. Then she turned her traitorous head and called 'Jim!' into the cottage.

A sleepy grunt rewarded her.

'Jim, I say!' she repeated. 'Come here directly a minute.'

Next moment Jim appeared. He was Jim to her because she was his wife, I suppose, but to us he was the Police, with his hair ruffled – from his hateful sofa-cushions, no doubt – and his tunic unbuttoned.

'What's up?' he said in a husky voice, as if he had been dreaming that he had a cold. 'Can't a chap have a minute to himself to read the paper in?'

'You told me to,' said the woman. 'You said if any folks come to the door with things I was to call you, whether or no.'

Even now we were blind to the disaster that was entangling us in the meshes of its trap. Alice said –

'We've sold a good deal, but we've *some* things left – very nice things. These crochet needles –'

But the Police, who had buttoned up his tunic in a hurry, said quite fiercely –

'Let's have a look at your licence.'

'We didn't bring any,' said Noël, 'but if you will give us an order we'll bring you some to-morrow.' He thought a lisen was a thing to sell that we ought to have thought of.

'None of your lip,' was the unexpected reply of the now plainly brutal constable. 'Where's your licence, I say?'

'We have a licence for our dog, but Father's got it,' said Oswald, always quick-witted, but not, this time, quite quick enough.

'Your 'awker's licence is what I want, as well you knows, you young limb. Your pedlar's licence – your licence to sell things. You ain't half so half-witted as you want to make out.'

'We haven't got a pedlar's licence,' said Oswald. If we had been in a book the Police would have been touched to tears by Oswald's simply honesty. He would have said 'Noble boy!' and then gone on to say he had only asked the question to test our honour. But life is not really at all the same as books. I have noticed lots of differences. Instead of behaving like the book-Police, this thick-headed constable said –

'Blowed if I wasn't certain of it! Well, my young blokes, you'll just come along o' me to Sir James. I've got orders to bring up the next case afore him.'

'Case!' said Dora. 'Oh, don't! We didn't know we oughtn't to. We only wanted –'

'Ho, yes,' said the constable, 'you can tell all that to the magistrate; and anything you say will be used against you.'

'I'm sure it will,' said Oswald. 'Dora, don't lower yourself to speak to him. Come, we'll go home.'

The Police was combing its hair with a half-toothless piece of comb, and we turned to go. But it was vain.

Ere any of our young and eager legs could climb into the cart the Police had seized the donkey's bridle. We could not desert our noble steed – and besides, it wasn't really ours, but Bates's, and this made any hope of flight quite a forlorn one. For better, for worse, we had to go with the donkey.

'Don't cry, for goodness' sake!' said Oswald in stern undertones. 'Bite your lips. Take long breaths. Don't let him see we mind. This beast's only the village police. Sir James will be a gentleman. *He'll* understand. Don't disgrace the house of Bastable. Look here! Fall into line – no, Indian file will be best, there are so few of us. Alice, if you snivel I'll never say you ought to have been a boy again. H.O., shut your mouth; no one's going to hurt you – you're too young.'

'I *am* trying,' said Alice, gasping.

'Noël,' Oswald went on – now, as so often, showing the brilliant qualities of the born leader and general – 'Don't *you* be in a funk. Remember how Byron fought for the Greeks at Missy-what's-its-name. *He* didn't grouse, and he was a poet, like you! Now look here, let's be *game*. Dora, you're the eldest. Strike up – any tune. We'll *march* up, and show this sneak we Bastables aren't afraid, whoever else is.'

You will perhaps find it difficult to believe, but we *did* strike up. We sang 'The British Grenadiers', and when the Police told us to stow it we did not. And Noël said –

'Singing isn't dogs or pedlaring. You don't want a licence for that.'

'I'll soon show you!' said the Police.

But he had to jolly well put up with our melodious song, because he knew that there isn't really any law to prevent you singing if you want to.

We went on singing. It soon got easier than at first, and we followed Bates's donkey and cart through some lodge gates and up a drive with big trees, and we came out in front of a big white house, and there was a lawn. We stopped singing when we came in sight of the house, and got ready to be polite to Sir James. There were some ladies on the lawn in pretty blue and green dresses. This cheered us. Ladies are seldom quite heartless, especially when young.

The Police drew up Bates's donkey opposite the big front door with pillars, and rang the bell. Our hearts were beating desperately. We cast glances of despair at the ladies. Then, quite suddenly, Alice gave a yell that wild Indian war-whoops are simply nothing to, and tore across the lawn and threw her arms round the green waist of one of the ladies.

'Oh, I'm so glad!' she cried; 'oh, save us! We haven't done anything wrong, really and truly we haven't.'

And then we all saw that the lady was our own Mrs Red House, that we liked so much. So we all rushed to her, and before that Police had got the door answered we had told her our tale. The other ladies had turned away when we approached her, and gone politely away into a shrubbery.

'There, there,' she said, patting Alice and Noël and as much of the others as she could get hold of. 'Don't you worry, dears, don't. I'll make it all right with Sir James. Let's all sit down in a comfy heap, and get our breaths again. I am so glad to see you all. My husband met your father at lunch the other day. I meant to come over and see you to-morrow.'

You cannot imagine the feelings of joy and safeness that we felt now we had found someone who knew we were Bastables, and not vagrant outcasts like the Police thought.

The door had now been answered. We saw the base Police talking to the person who answered it. Then he came towards us, very red in the face.

'Leave off bothering the lady,' he said, 'and come along of me. Sir James is in his library, and he's ready to do justice on you, so he is.'

Mrs Red House jumped up, and so did we. She said with smiles, as if nothing was wrong –

'Good morning, Inspector!'

He looked pleased and surprised, as well he might, for it'll be long enough before he's within a mile of being *that*.

'Good morning, miss, I'm sure,' he replied.

'I think there's been a little mistake, Inspector,' she said. 'I expect it's some of your men – led away by zeal for their duties. But I'm sure *you'll* understand. I am staying with Lady Harborough, and these children are very dear friends of mine.'

The Police looked very silly, but he said something about hawking without a licence.

'Oh no, not *hawking*,' said Mrs Red House, 'not *hawking*, surely! They were just *playing* at it, you know. Your subordinates must have been quite mistaken.'

Our honesty bade us say that he was his own only subordinate, and that he hadn't been mistaken; but it is rude to interrupt, especially a lady, so we said nothing.

The Police said firmly, 'You'll excuse me, miss, but Sir James expressly told me to lay on information directly next time I caught any of 'em at it without a licence.'

'But, you see, you didn't catch them at it.' Mrs Red House took some money out of her purse. 'You might just give this to your subordinates to console them for the mistake they've made. And look here, these mistakes do lead to trouble sometimes. So I'll tell you what I'll do. I'll promise not to tell Sir James a word about it. *So* nobody will be blamed.'

We listened breathless for his reply. He put his hands behind him –

'Well, miss,' he said at last, 'you've managed to put the Force in the wrong somehow, which isn't often done, and I'm blest if I know how you make it out. But there's Sir James a-waiting for me to come before him with my complaint. What am I a-goin' to say to him?'

'Oh, anything,' said Mrs Red House; 'surely some one

else has done something wrong that you can tell him about?'

'There was a matter of a couple of snares and some night lines,' he said slowly, drawing nearer to Mrs Red House; 'but I couldn't take no money, of course.'

'Of course not,' she said; 'I beg your pardon for offering it. But I'll give you my name and address, and if ever I can be of any use to you –'

She turned her back on us while she wrote it down with a stumpy pencil he lent her; but Oswald could swear that he heard money chink, and that there was something large and round wrapped up in the paper she gave him.

'Sorry for any little misunderstanding,' the Police now said, feeling the paper with his fingers; 'and my respects to you, miss, and your young friends. I'd best be going.'

And he went – to Sir James, I suppose. He seemed quite tamed. I hope the people who set the snares got off.

'So *that's* all right,' said Mrs Red House. 'Oh, you dear children, you must stay to lunch, and we'll have a splendid time.'

'What a darling Princess you are!' Noël said slowly. 'You are a witch Princess, too, with magic powers over the Police.'

'It's not a very pretty sort of magic,' she said, and she sighed.

'Everything about you is pretty,' said Noël. And I could see him beginning to make the faces that always precur his poetry-fits. But before the fit could break out thoroughly the rest of us awoke from our stupor of grateful safeness and began to dance round Mrs Red House in a ring. And the girls sang –

> *'The rose is red, the violet's blue,*
> *Carnation's sweet, and so are you,'*

over and over again, so we had to join in; though I think 'She's a jolly good fellow' would have been more manly and less like a poetry book.

Suddenly a known voice broke in on our singing.

'*Well!*' it said. And we stopped dancing. And there were the other two ladies who had politely walked off when we first discovered Mrs Red House. And one of them was Mrs Bax – of all people in the world! And she was smoking a cigarette. So now we knew where the smell of tobacco came from, in the White House.

We said, '*Oh!*' in one breath, and were silent.

'Is it possible,' said Mrs Bax, 'that these are the Sunday-school children I've been living with these three long days?'

'We're sorry,' said Dora, softly; 'we wouldn't have made a noise if we'd known you were here.'

'So I suppose,' said Mrs Bax. 'Chloe, you seem to be a witch. How have you galvanized my six rag dolls into life like this?'

'Rag dolls!' said H.O., before we could stop him. 'I think you're jolly mean and ungrateful; and it was sixpence for making the organs fly.'

'My brain's reeling,' said Mrs Bax, putting her hands to her head.

'H.O. is very rude, and I am sorry,' said Alice, 'but it *is* hard to be called rag dolls, when you've only tried to do as you were told.'

And then, in answer to Mrs Red House's questions, we told how father had begged us to be quiet, and how we had earnestly tried to. When it was told, Mrs Bax began to laugh, and so did Mrs Red House, and at last Mrs Bax said –

'Oh, my dears! you don't know how glad I am that you're really alive! I began to think – oh – I don't know what I thought! And you're not rag dolls. You're heroes and heroines, every man jack of you. And I do thank you. But I never wanted to be quiet like *that*. I just didn't want to be bothered with London and tiresome grown-up people. And now let's enjoy ourselves! Shall it be rounders, or stories about cannibals?'

'Rounders first and stories after,' said H.O. And it was so.

Mrs Bax, now that her true nature was revealed, proved to be A1. The author does not ask for a jollier person to be in the house with. We had rare larks the whole time she stayed with us.

And to think that we might never have known her true character if she hadn't been an old school friend of Mrs Red House's, and if Mrs Red House hadn't been such a friend of ours!

'Friendship,' as Mr William Smith so truly says in his book about Latin, 'is the crown of life.'

THE POOR AND NEEDY

'WHAT shall we do to-day, kiddies?' said Mrs Bax. We had discovered her true nature but three days ago, and already she had taken us out in a sailing-boat and in a motor car, had given us sweets every day, and taught us eleven new games that we had not known before; and only four of the new games were rotters. How seldom can as much be said for the games of a grown-up, however gifted!

The day was one of cloudless blue perfectness, and we were all basking on the beach. We had all bathed. Mrs Bax said we might. There are points about having a grown-up with you, if it is the right kind. You can then easily get it to say 'Yes' to what you want, and after that, if anything goes wrong it is their fault, and you are pure from blame. But nothing had gone wrong with the bathe, and, so far, we were all alive, and not cold at all, except our fingers and feet.

'What would you *like* to do?' asked Mrs Bax. We were far away from human sight along the beach, and Mrs Bax was smoking cigarettes as usual.

'I don't know,' we all said politely. But H.O. said –

'What about poor Miss Sandal?'

'Why poor?' asked Mrs Bax.

'Because she is,' said H.O.

'But how? What do you mean?' asked Mrs Bax.

'Why, isn't she?' said H.O.

'Isn't she what?' said Mrs Bax.

'What you said why about,' said H.O.

She put her hands to her head. Her short hair was still

damp and rumpled from contact with the foaming billows of ocean.

'Let's have a fresh deal and start fair,' she said; 'why do you think my sister is poor?'

'I forgot she was your sister,' said H.O., 'or I wouldn't have said it – honour bright I wouldn't.'

'Don't mention it,' said Mrs Bax, and began throwing stones at a groin in amiable silence.

We were furious with H.O., first because it is such bad manners to throw people's poverty in their faces, or even in their sisters' faces, like H.O. had just done, and second because it seemed to have put out of Mrs Bax's head what she was beginning to say about what would we like to do.

So Oswald presently remarked, when he had aimed at the stump she was aiming at, and hit it before she did, for though a fair shot for a lady, she takes a long time to get her eye in.

'Mrs Bax, we should like to do whatever *you* like to do.' This was real politeness and true too, as it happened, because by this time we could quite trust her not to want to do anything deeply duffing.

'That's very nice of you,' she replied, 'but don't let me interfere with any plans of yours. My own idea was to pluck a waggonette from the nearest bush. I suppose they grow freely in these parts?'

'There's one at the "Ship",' said Alice; 'it costs seven-and-six to pluck it, just for going to the station.'

'Well, then! And to stuff our waggonette with lunch and drive over to Lynwood Castle, and eat it there.'

'A picnic!' fell in accents of joy from the lips of one and all.

'We'll also boil the billy in the castle courtyard, and eat buns in the shadow of the keep.'

'Tea as well?' said H.O., 'with buns? You can't be poor and needy any way, whatever your –'

We hastily hushed him, stifling his murmurs with sand.

'I always think,' said Mrs Bax dreamily, 'that "the more the merrier" is peculiarly true of picnics. So I have arranged – always subject to your approval, of course – to meet your friends, Mr and Mrs Red House, there, and –'

We drowned her conclusive remarks with a cheer. And Oswald, always willing to be of use, offered to go to the 'Ship' and see about the waggonette. I like horses and stable-yards, and the smell of hay and straw, and talking to ostlers and people like that.

There turned out to be two horses belonging to the best waggonette, or you could have a one-horse one, much smaller, with the blue cloth of the cushions rather frayed, and mended here and there, and green in patches from age and exposition to the weather.

Oswald told Mrs Bax this, not concealing about how shabby the little one was, and she gloriously said –

'The pair by all means! We don't kill a pig every day!'

'No, indeed,' said Dora, but if 'killing a pig' means having a lark, Mrs Bax is as good a pig-killer as any I ever knew.

It was splendid to drive (Oswald, on the box beside the driver, who had his best coat with the bright buttons) along the same roads that we had trodden as muddy pedestrinators, or travelled along behind Bates's donkey.

It was a perfect day, as I said before. We were all clean and had our second-best things on. I think second-bests are much more comfy than first-bests. You feel equivalent to meeting any one, and have 'a heart for any fate', as it says in the poetry-book, and yet you are not starched and booted and stiffened and tightened out of all human feelings.

Lynwood Castle is in a hollow in the hills. It has a moat all round it with water-lily leaves on it. I suppose there are lilies when in season. There is a bridge over the moat – not the draw kind of bridge. And the castle has eight towers – four round and four square ones, and a courtyard in the middle, all green grass, and heaps of stones – stray bits of castle, I suppose they are – and a great white may-tree in the middle that Mrs Bax said was hundreds of years old.

Mrs Red House was sitting under the may-tree when we got there, nursing her baby, in a blue dress and looking exactly like a picture on the top of a chocolate-box.

The girls instantly wanted to nurse the baby so we let them. And we explored the castle. We had never happened to explore one thoroughly before. We did not find the deepest dungeon below the castle moat, though we looked everywhere for it, but we found everything else you can think of belonging to castles – even the holes they used to pour boiling lead through into the eyes of besiegers when they tried to squint up to see how strong the garrison was in the keep – and the little slits they shot arrows through, and the mouldering remains of the portcullis. We went up the eight towers, every single one of them, and some parts were jolly dangerous, I can tell you. Dicky and I would not let H.O. and Noël come up the dangerous parts. There was no lasting ill-feeling about this. By the time we had had a thorough good explore lunch was ready.

It was a glorious lunch – not too many meaty things, but all sorts of cakes and sweets, and grapes and figs and nuts.

We gazed at the feast, and Mrs Bax said –

'There you are, young Copperfield, and a royal spread you've got.'

'*They* had currant wine,' said Noël, who has only just read the book by Mr Charles Dickens.

'Well, so have you,' said Mrs Bax. And we had. Two bottles of it.

'I never knew any one like you,' said Noël to Mrs Red House, dreamily with his mouth full, 'for knowing the things people really like to eat, not the things that are good for them, but what they *like*, and Mrs Bax is just the same.'

'It was one of the things they taught at our school,' said

Mrs Bax. 'Do you remember the Saturday night feasts, Chloe, and how good the cocoanut ice tasted after extra strong peppermints?'

'Fancy you knowing *that*!' said H.O. 'I thought it was us found *that* out.'

'I really know much more about things to eat than *she* does,' said Mrs Bax. 'I was quite an old girl when she was a little thing in pinafores. She was such a nice little girl.'

'I shouldn't wonder if she was always nice,' said Noël, 'even when she was a baby!'

Everybody laughed at this, except the existing baby, and it was asleep on the waggonette cushions, under the white may-tree, and perhaps if it had been awake it wouldn't have laughed, for Oswald himself, though possessing a keen sense of humour, did not see anything to laugh at.

Mr Red House made a speech after dinner, and said drink to the health of everybody, one after the other, in currant wine, which was done, beginning with Mrs Bax and ending with H.O.

Then he said –

'Somnus, avaunt! What shall we play at?' and nobody, as so often happens, had any idea ready. Then suddenly Mrs Red House said –

'Good gracious, look there!' and we looked there, and where we were to look was the lowest piece of the castle wall, just beside the keep that the bridge led over to, and what we were to look at was a strange blobbiness of knobbly bumps along the top, that looked exactly like human heads.

It turned out, when we had talked about cannibals and New Guinea, that human heads were just exactly what they were. Not loose heads, stuck on pikes or things like that, such as there often must have been while the castle stayed in the olden times it was built in and belonged to, but real live heads with their bodies still in attendance on them.

They were, in fact, the village children.

'Poor little Lazaruses!' said Mr Red House.

'There's not such a bad slice of Dives' feast left,' said Mrs Bax. 'Shall we –?'

So Mr Red House went out by the keep and called the heads in (with the bodies they were connected with, of course), and they came and ate up all that was left of the lunch. Not the buns, of course, for those were sacred to tea-time, but all the other things, even the nuts and figs, and we were quite glad that they should have them – really and truly we were, even H.O.!

They did not seem to be very clever children, or just the sort you would choose for your friends, but I suppose you like to play, however little you are other people's sort. So, after they had eaten all there was, when Mrs Red House invited them all to join in games with us we knew we ought to be pleased. But village children are not taught rounders, and though we wondered at first why their teachers had not seen to this, we understood presently. Because it is most awfully difficult to make them understand the very simplest thing.

But they could play all the ring games, and 'Nuts and May' and 'There Came Three Knights' – and another one we had never heard of before. The singing part begins: –

> *Up and down the green grass,*
> *This and that and thus,*
> *Come along, my pretty maid,*
> *And take a walk with us.*
> *You shall have a duck, my dear,*
> *And you shall have a drake,*
> *And you shall have a handsome man*
> *For your father's sake.*

I forget the rest, and if anybody who reads this knows it, and will write and tell me, the author will not have laboured in vain.

The grown-ups played with all their heart and soul – I expect it is but seldom they are able to play, and they enjoy the novel excitement. And when we'd been at it some time we saw there was another head looking over the wall.

'Hullo!' said Mrs Bax, 'here's another of them, run along and ask it to come and join in.'

She spoke to the village children, but nobody ran.

'Here, you go,' she said, pointing at a girl in red plaits tied with dirty sky-blue ribbon.

'Please, miss, I'd leifer not,' replied the red-haired. 'Mother says we ain't to play along of him.'

'Why, what's the matter with him?' asked Mrs Red House.

'His father's in jail, miss, along of snares and night lines, and no one won't give his mother any work, so my mother says we ain't to demean ourselves to speak to him.'

'But it's not the child's fault,' said Mrs Red House, 'is it now?'

'I don't know, miss,' said the red-haired.

'But it's cruel,' said Mrs Bax. 'How would you like it if your father was sent to prison, and nobody would speak to you?'

'Father's always kep' hisself respectable,' said the girl with the dirty blue ribbon. 'You can't be sent to jail, not if you keeps yourself respectable, you can't, miss.'

'And do none of you speak to him?'

The other children put their fingers in their mouths, and looked silly, showing plainly that they didn't.

'Don't you feel sorry for the poor little chap?' said Mrs Bax.

No answer transpired.

'Can't you imagine how you'd feel if it was *your* father?'

'My father always kep' hisself respectable,' the red-haired girl said again.

'Well, I shall ask him to come and play with us,' said Mrs

Red House. 'Little pigs!' she added in low tones only heard by the author and Mr Red House.

But Mr Red House said in a whisper that no one overheard except Mrs R. H. and the present author.

'Don't, Puss-cat; it's no good. The poor little pariah wouldn't like it. And these kids only do what their parents teach them.'

If the author didn't know what a stainless gentleman Mr Red House is he would think he heard him mutter a word that gentlemen wouldn't say.

'Tell off a detachment of consolation,' Mr Red House went on; 'look here, *our* kids – who'll go and talk to the poor little chap?'

We all instantly said, '*I* will!'

The present author was chosen to be the one.

When you think about yourself there is a kind of you that is not what you generally are but that you know you would like to be if only you were good enough. Albert's uncle says this is called your ideal of yourself. I will call it your best I, for short. Oswald's 'best I' was glad to go and talk to that boy whose father was in prison, but the Oswald that generally exists hated being out of the games. Yet the whole Oswald, both the best and the ordinary, was pleased that he was the one chosen to be a detachment of consolation.

He went out under the great archway, and as he went he heard the games beginning again. This made him feel noble, and yet he was ashamed of feeling it. Your feelings are a beastly nuisance, if once you begin to let yourself think about them. Oswald soon saw the broken boots of the boy whose father was in jail so nobody would play with him, standing on the stones near the top of the wall where it was broken to match the boots.

He climbed up and said, 'Hullo!'

To this remark the boy replied, 'Hullo!'

Oswald now did not know what to say. The sorrier you are for people the harder it is to tell them so.

But at last he said –

'I've just heard about your father being where he is. It's beastly rough luck. I hope you don't mind my saying I'm jolly sorry for you.'

The boy had a pale face and watery blue eyes. When Oswald said this his eyes got waterier than ever, and he climbed down to the ground before he said –

'I don't care so much, but it do upset mother something crool.'

It is awfully difficult to console those in affliction. Oswald thought this, then he said –

'I say; never mind if those beastly kids won't play with you. It isn't your fault, you know.'

'Nor it ain't father's neither,' the boy said; 'he broke his arm a-falling off of a rick, and he hadn't paid up his club money along of mother's new baby costing what it did when it come, so there warn't nothing – and what's a hare or two, or a partridge? It ain't as if it was pheasants as is as dear to rear as chicks.'

Oswald did not know what to say, so he got out his new pen-and-pencil-combined and said –

'Look here! You can have this to keep if you like.'

The pale-eyed boy took it and looked at it and said –

'You ain't foolin' me?'

And Oswald said no he wasn't, but he felt most awfully rum and uncomfy, and though he wanted most frightfully to do something for the boy he felt as if he wanted to get away more than anything else, and he never was gladder in his life than when he saw Dora coming along, and she said –

'You go back and play, Oswald. I'm tired and I'd like to sit down a bit.'

She got the boy to sit down beside her, and Oswald went back to the others.

Games, however unusually splendid, have to come to an
end. And when the games were over and it was tea, and the
village children were sent away, and Oswald went to call
Dora and the prisoner's son, he found nothing but Dora,
and he saw at once, in his far-sighted way, that she had been
crying.

It was one of the A1est days we ever had, and the drive
home was good, but Dora was horribly quiet, as though the
victim of dark interior thoughts.

And the next day she was but little better.

We were all paddling on the sands, but Dora would not.
And presently Alice left us and went back to Dora, and we
all saw across the sandy waste that something was up.

And presently Alice came down and said –

'Dry your feet and legs and come to a council. Dora wants
to tell you something.'

We dried our pink and sandy toes and we came to the
council. Then Alice said: 'I don't think H.O. is wanted at
the council, it isn't anything amusing; you go and enjoy
yourself by the sea, and catch the nice little crabs, H.O.
dear.'

H.O. said: 'You always want me to be out of everything. I
can be councils as well as anybody else.'

'Oh, H.O.!' said Alice, in pleading tones, 'not if I give
you a halfpenny to go and buy bulls-eyes with?'

So then he went, and Dora said –

'I can't think how I could do it when you'd all trusted me
so. And yet I couldn't help it. I remember Dicky saying
when you decided to give it me to take care of – about me
being the most trustworthy of all of us. I'm not fit for any
one to speak to. But it did seem the really right thing at the
time, it really and truly did. And now it all looks different.'

'What has she done?' Dicky asked this, but Oswald
almost knew.

'Tell them,' said Dora, turning over on her front and

hiding her face partly in her hands, and partly in the sand.

'She's given all Miss Sandal's money to that little boy that the father of was in prison,' said Alice.

'It was one pound thirteen and sevenpence halfpenny,' sobbed Dora.

'You ought to have consulted us, I do think, really,' said Dicky. 'Of course, I see you're sorry now, but I do think that.'

'How could I consult you?' said Dora; 'you were all playing Cat and Mouse, and he wanted to get home. I only wish you'd heard what he told me – that's all – about his mother being ill, and nobody letting her do any work because of where his father is, and his baby brother ill, poor little darling, and not enough to eat, and everything as awful as you can possibly think. I'll save up and pay it all back out of my own money. Only do forgive me, all of you, and say you don't despise me for a forger and embezzlementer. I couldn't help it.'

'I'm glad you couldn't,' said the sudden voice of H.O., who had sneaked up on his young stomach unobserved by the council. 'You shall have all my money too, Dora, and here's the bulls-eye halfpenny to begin with.' He crammed it into her hand. 'Listen? I should jolly well think I did listen,' H.O. went on. 'I've just as much right as anybody else to be in at a council, and I think Dora was quite right, and the rest of you are beasts not to say so, too, when you see how she's blubbing. Suppose it had been *your* darling baby-brother ill, and nobody hadn't given you nothing when they'd got pounds and pounds in their silly pockets?'

He now hugged Dora, who responded.

'It wasn't her own money,' said Dicky.

'If you think *you're* our darling baby-brother –' said Oswald.

But Alice and Noël began hugging Dora and H.O., and Dicky and I felt it was no go. Girls have no right and honourable feelings about business, and little boys are the same.

'All right,' said Oswald rather bitterly, 'if a majority of the council backs Dora up, we'll give in. But we must all save up and repay the money, that's all. We shall all be beastly short for ages.'

'Oh,' said Dora, and now her sobs were beginning to turn into sniffs, 'you don't know how I felt! And I've felt most awful ever since, but those poor, poor people –'

At this moment Mrs Bax came down on to the beach by the wooden steps that lead from the sea-wall where the grass grows between the stones.

'Hullo!' she said, 'hurt yourself, my Dora-dove?'

Dora was rather a favourite of hers.

'It's all right now,' said Dora.

'*That's* all right,' said Mrs Bax, who has learnt in anti-what's-its-name climes the great art of not asking too many questions. 'Mrs Red House has come to lunch. She went this morning to see the boy's mother – you know, the boy the others wouldn't play with?'

We said 'Yes.'

'Well, Mrs Red House has arranged to get the woman some work – like the dear she is – the woman told her that the little lady – and that's you, Dora – had given the little boy one pound thirteen and sevenpence.'

Mrs Bax looked straight out to sea through her gold-rimmed spectacles, and went on –

'That must have been about all you had among the lot of you. I don't want to jaw, but I think you're a set of little bricks, and I must say so or expire on the sandy spot.'

There was a painful silence.

H.O. looked, 'There, what did I tell you?' at the rest of us.

Then Alice said, 'We others had nothing to do with it. It was Dora's doing.' I suppose she said this because we did not mean to tell Mrs Bax anything about it, and if there was any brickiness in the act we wished Dora to have the consolement of getting the credit of it.

But of course Dora couldn't stand that. She said –

'Oh, Mrs Bax, it was very wrong of me. It wasn't my own money, and I'd no business to, but I was so sorry for the little boy and his mother and his darling baby-brother. The money belonged to some one else.'

'Who?' Mrs Bax asked ere she had time to remember the excellent Australian rule about not asking questions.

And H.O. blurted out, 'It was Miss Sandal's money – every penny,' before we could stop him.

Once again in our career concealment was at an end. The rule about questions was again unregarded, and the whole thing came out.

It was a long story, and Mrs Red House came out in the middle, but nobody could mind her hearing things.

When she knew all, from the plain living to the pedlar who hadn't a licence, Mrs Bax spoke up like a man, and said several kind things that I won't write down.

She then went on to say that her sister was not poor and needy at all, but that she lived plain and thought high just because she liked it!

We were very disappointed as soon as we had got over our hardly believing any one could – like it, I mean – and then Mrs Red House said –

'Sir James gave me five pounds for the poor woman, and she sent back thirty of your shillings. She had spent three and sevenpence, and they had a lovely supper of boiled pork and greens last night. So now you've only got that to make up, and you can buy a most splendid present for Miss Sandal.'

It is difficult to choose presents for people who live plain and think high because they like it. But at last we decided to get books. They were written by a person called Emerson, and of a dull character, but the backs were very beautiful, and Miss Sandal was most awfully pleased with them when she came down to her cottage with her partially repaired brother, who had fallen off the scaffold when treating a bricklayer to tracts.

This is the end of the things we did when we were at Lymchurch in Miss Sandal's house.

It is the last story that the present author means ever to be the author of. So goodbye, if you have got as far as this.

Your affectionate author,

OSWALD BASTABLE.

Other Puffins by E. Nesbit

THE STORY OF THE TREASURE SEEKERS
THE ENCHANTED CASTLE
THE WOULDBEGOODS
THE LAST OF THE DRAGONS AND SOME
OTHERS
THE RAILWAY CHILDREN
FIVE CHILDREN AND IT
THE STORY OF THE AMULET
THE PHOENIX AND THE CARPET

Heard about the Puffin Club?

... it's a way of finding out more about Puffin books and authors, of winning prizes (in competitions), sharing jokes, a secret code, and perhaps seeing your name in print! When you join you get a copy of our magazine, *Puffin Post*, sent to you four times a year, a badge and a membership book.

For details of subscription and an application form, send a stamped addressed envelope to:

The Puffin Club Dept A
Penguin Books Limited
Bath Road
Harmondsworth
Middlesex UB7 0DA

and if you live in Australia, please write to:

The Australian Puffin Club
Penguin Books Australia Limited
P.O. Box 257
Ringwood
Victoria 3134